CLARINET TECHNIQUE

Clarinet Technique

BY

FREDERICK THURSTON

Third edition

London   Oxford   New York

OXFORD UNIVERSITY PRESS

1977

Oxford University Press, Walton Street, Oxford OX2 6DP

OXFORD LONDON GLASGOW NEW YORK TORONTO MELBOURNE
WELLINGTON CAPE TOWN IBADAN NAIROBI DAR ES SALAAM
LUSAKA DELHI BOMBAY CALCUTTA MADRAS KARACHI LAHORE
DACCA KUALA LUMPUR SINGAPORE HONG KONG TOKYO

ISBN 0 19 318610 1

Third edition © Oxford University Press 1977

First edition 1956
Second edition 1964
Third edition 1977

*Printed in Great Britain by
The Camelot Press Ltd, Southampton*

CONTENTS

ACKNOWLEDGEMENTS

The illustrations showing correct and incorrect positions of the clarinet in the mouth are based, by permission, on an illustration which appeared in an article by Mr. Maurice M. Porter in the *British Dental Journal* of 5 August 1952.

The extract from Ravel's Septet is reproduced by permission of Durand & Cie., Paris (United Music Publishers, London); from Rimsky-Korsakov's *Coq d'Or* by permission of Rob. Forbert (Agents: Novello & Co. Ltd.); from Prokofiev's *Peter and the Wolf*, Rimsky-Korsakov's *Scheherazade*, and Gerald Finzi's Clarinet Concerto by permission of Boosey & Hawkes Ltd., the last-named work by permission also of Mr. Finzi; from Hindemith's Clarinet Concerto by permission of Schott & Co.; and from Elizabeth Maconchy's Clarinet Concertino by permission of Miss Maconchy.

FOREWORD

'The Clarinet has long been considered by the whole Musical Profession as the most beautiful of Wind Instruments. On the Continent it is very generally cultivated, nor is it improbable that in the course of a few years its merits will procure for it an equal degree of attachment from English Amateurs; for surely a Tone that nearly rivals the finest human Voice, and an extent of Octaves that may vie even with the ample range of the Violin, are excellencies that *must* at no very distant period share a considerable portion of popularity.'

So began Thomas Willman's *Instruction Book for the Clarinet* in 1825, and his prophecy has been more than fulfilled. Despite the many mechanical improvements the clarinet has enjoyed since his time, the aim of every player should still be, as Willman took pains to show, to develop a technique in order to serve his musical expression, and not as an end in itself. Anyone can, with diligent application, learn to control the mechanism of a clarinet; not everyone can play music on it. The former is no more than an efficient mechanic. Your technique must be good only because if it is not your musical expression will be impeded. There is no other reason for technique. Tone production, tongue and finger efficiency, choice of reed, and transposition are all a part of it, whether you are aspiring to play the clarinet, bass clarinet, basset horn, or saxophone; whether you intend to take part in chamber music, or to play in a symphony orchestra, a dance band, or a military band.

Even if you do not intend to become a professional, your enjoyment, and that of others, will be enhanced by technical efficiency. The adjective 'amateurish' should not imply 'incompetent'. The true amateur, in the dictionary sense of the word, is one who cultivates a particular study or art for the love of it; he is prepared to take trouble to be master of his hobby, and he is never despised by the best professional artists.

This book does not pretend to take the place of personal

supervision by a teacher; it can only give you the fundamental principles, perhaps in more detail than the average
space of the tutor or instruction book allows. It may be
helpful for those who cannot easily get first-hand instruction, but it should be used mainly to supplement your
lessons. Some regular tuition is essential if you hope to
become a fine player, if only because it is impossible to
describe on paper anything to do with beauty of sound.

Though the chapters may be taken in any order by more
advanced players, they may be followed straight through
by beginners. This order also corresponds roughly to the
ideal programme for a day's practice, although some of
its chapters are inseparable—for instance, those on tone
production and breathing, or articulation and staccato.
To avoid complication over fingerings for the various systems of clarinet still used, I have presumed that the player
has a chart to suit his instrument. A few of the remarks
apply to the Boehm only, as it is the most widely known,
but most of the examples should be workable on any
system.

NOTE ON THE FIRST EDITION

The author of this book died while the MS. was in its final
stages, and the publisher wishes to express his grateful
thanks to Miss Thea King and Mr. John Warrack for
their help in preparing the book for the printer and seeing
it into print.

NOTE ON THE THIRD EDITION

For this edition I have been through the text and amended
where this seemed called for. I am grateful to Alan Hacker
and John Davies for their contributions, and deeply appreciate Georgina Dobrée's work in completely recompiling the
List of Music.

Thea King

I

THE BEGINNINGS—TONE

You have chosen to play the clarinet because you are attracted to it and have a desire to produce yourself its particular kind of tone quality. All the books, all the articles and technical advice in the world are of little use unless you have in your 'mind's ear' the particular sound you wish to make. Presumably you will have decided this by listening to various fine players, if possible at public performances, because even nowadays the radio and the gramophone cannot reproduce tone quality completely faithfully. The nationality of the player or the make of instrument has little to do with it, whatever you may hear said; there are only two kinds of sound, good and bad.

Having selected what you think will be a satisfactory combination of reed and mouthpiece (see Appendices I and II) the first step is the foundation of a good embouchure, or necessary formation of the mouth, which includes the position and control of the jaws, lips, teeth, and surrounding muscles. The following remarks assume that you are a beginner, but even if you are not, it is a good plan to hark back occasionally over these preliminary points in the continual desire to improve your tone.

(a) Stand up straight with the body thoroughly relaxed, feet slightly apart, and head erect, looking straight ahead. It is best to play as much as possible standing up, but if you do have to sit down make sure that you adopt as upright a position as possible. Do not rest the bell of the clarinet on the knee as this is bad for the control of embouchure, fingers, and breath. Rather than resort to a sitting position because you are tired from playing, it is better to abandon practice until you are completely fresh, at any rate in the early stages. You will find, too, that a number of short spells of practice with short rests will keep you fresher than going on until you begin to tire and then resting until you feel ready to begin again. Five-minute periods will probably be found quite long enough at the very beginning: you will find your endurance developing of its own accord with time. But do not on any account over-practice: you cannot concentrate when you are physically and mentally tired, and you will do your playing as much harm as by not practising at all.

(b) Hold the clarinet with the right-hand thumb under the thumb-rest and the fingers of that hand resting against the rod attached to the rings. The left hand can be used to steady the instrument by holding the barrel. To produce the open note, G, none of the finger-holes need be covered. The elbows should neither be pressed against the body nor held out stiffly, but allowed to fall naturally. Positions of embouchure and stance obviously differ from one player to another, but the clarinet should make an angle of about 40° with the body.

(c) Put the tip of the mouthpiece between the almost closed lips and rest the reed on the bottom lip. Now gently push the instrument into the mouth so that the lower lip is drawn over the bottom teeth. Meanwhile let the top teeth rest lightly on the mouthpiece and close the lip around them, which will prevent any breath escaping when you actually blow. This shows you how to form the embouchure; so far you have produced no sound.

(d) First you must find out how much of the mouthpiece should be in the mouth to allow the reed to vibrate freely and give the fullest tone. So take a good[1] breath and then repeat (c), meanwhile blowing gently without puffing out the cheeks. At first you will get no sound at all, but as you push more mouthpiece into the mouth the note will suddenly come. Experiment gently with this, and you will find that there is a position which gives the most satisfactory sound. There should be a fair amount of pressure of the reed downwards on to the bottom lip. Now compare the position (in a mirror) with the diagram, which shows the average amount taken into the mouth by most first-class players. Practise this until you can take up the embouchure position quickly and comfortably. The sound

[1] For a fuller exposition of the problems of breathing and breath control see Chap. II.

you make at first may not be very pleasant, possibly for one of the following reasons:

(i) The reed may not be pressing firmly enough on the bottom lip. Your left hand, which is holding the barrel, can be used to test and adjust this at first.

(ii) The muscles from the corners of the mouth to the cheeks should be contracted as if in a held smile, and there should be no air space between the inside of the cheeks and the back teeth.

(iii) When putting the instrument into your mouth, make sure that the clarinet goes to you, and not you to the

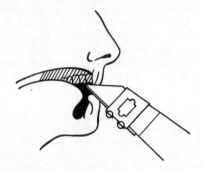

clarinet. Do not, for instance, take a sudden bite at the instrument.

(iv) Make sure, apropos the last point, that you are carefully following the instructions given in (c).

(v) Some players find it more comfortable to cover the upper teeth as well as the lower with the lip. There is nothing against this, but the other method is recommended as more generally satisfactory, and as being more likely to give an easy embouchure and consequently a good tone. The slightest change in position can make an enormous difference to the quality of the sound. You can only find out what suits you best by experiment. Obviously allowances must be made if you have protruding teeth, a very thick bottom lip, or a very long upper lip. There are sometimes instances of the teeth causing soreness or a cut lip. In extreme cases your dentist may help, but on no account resort to him without first consulting a clarinet teacher. There are a few dentists with a specialist interest in wind players' problems. You may also find that the bottom teeth make a groove inside the lip, especially if they are sharp, but this will become easier with time; meanwhile it is wise to play for only short spells at a time.

Because the reed vibrates inside the mouth the size and depth of the cavity (or resonating chamber) must have some bearing on the quality and quantity of the tone produced. There are certain natural physical characteristics which help to make a fine player on any instrument, and in this case the formation of teeth, lips, and jaw doubtless has some effect. Many people try to play instruments for which they are physically quite unsuited, but a glance at the physiognomy of a number of fine performers will show that there is no such thing as a 'clarinet face'.

Long notes

When you feel that you can produce a reasonable sound on the open note, G, take your left hand from the barrel and play F, one tone lower (see your fingering chart); then go on lower down the instrument, gradually adding one finger at a time. Do not remove the clarinet from the mouth between the notes in case you should disturb the ideal embouchure position you have found. (If you do take the instrument out of your mouth and look at your fingering, be careful not to catch the reed on your left shoulder.) Merely relax the lips and take a breath through the sides of the mouth (*not* through the instrument). Start each note as quietly as possible, i.e. breathe very gently into the clarinet, and gradually increase the intensity of breath until you reach fortissimo (see Chapter II). Then diminish the tone back to the opening whisper, listening carefully so that the pitch of the note does not alter from beginning to end. If you try to force the tone too much the quality will suffer, the pitch will drop, or an unpleasant squeak may occur. At first you may not be capable of much variation in dynamics or a very long sustained note, but practice will extend this; in fact, this is one of the exercises you should be prepared to practise all your life, listening continually for a beautiful quality of tone.

Some notes on every clarinet are weaker in quality than others, noticeably the A and B♭ immediately above open G, the so-called 'throat notes'. This is because the keys and holes used to produce them are the highest up, so that there is only a comparatively short column of air vibrating in the upper part of the tube. Therefore special attention should be paid to these when practising long notes. Covering some of the right-hand finger-holes can help to improve the tone, but it must not alter the pitch (unless this is purposely intended for intonation reasons). Try to imagine also that you are increasing the mouth cavity to give more resonance to the note as in a yawn.

Where it is possible, for instance on the Boehm system, an alternative fingering for B♭ often gives a better note. With the A key, instead of the speaker use the second of the four trill keys, played with the right-hand forefinger (halfway up the instrument). This is particularly suitable if the B♭ has to be sustained for any length of time. It is too awkward to reach to be practicable in fast passages, but then the thinness of tone will not be so apparent and the normal fingering can be used.

II

BREATH CONTROL

The principles of good breath control in clarinet playing are fundamentally the same as those used in singing, and they should be just as seriously considered by wind-players. Specialists in voice production have written countless books on the subject, which are interesting for the clarinettist to study. A knowledgeable, factual, and unusually clear exposition is Franklyn Kelsey's *The Foundations of Singing* and, amongst others, Keith Stein gives detailed help in his *Introduction to Clarinet Playing*.

The aim should be to breathe as naturally and uncon-sciously as possible, with no more concentration on the mechanism involved than is needed when idly humming a tune. Most players find that breath control develops automatically as they advance. It can be a mistake to give too much thought to it while actually playing, though you should understand the muscles used in order to be able to control them at will.

In the normal, rather sedentary, life which civilized man now leads the lungs and breathing muscles are not often called upon to work at their fullest extent, and one only becomes conscious of how they function when 'out of breath' after violent physical exercise. The inhalation and exhalation of air is controlled by a very important muscle called the diaphragm, and not by the lungs, as most people suppose. This may be compared to a large piece of elastic forming the floor of the chest cavity and separating it from the abdomen. In a relaxed position it arches upwards into a dome beneath the ribs, the highest point being in the centre, and the lowest at about waist level. When contracted downwards the floor of the chest is lowered and the volume of the cavity between the dia-phragm and the lungs enlarged. As this cavity has no outlet, a vacuum is formed, causing the lungs, suspended in the cavity, to fill out and correct the vacuum. As they fill out, they automatically draw in air from outside the body; this is simply what happens when you breathe in. Then as the diaphragm expands upwards the air is forced out again, although the lungs are never completely emptied.

To appreciate how this muscle works, place your hand against the triangle formed (in the front of the chest) just beneath where the two lowest ribs branch away. Now breathe in as though you were going to heave a deep sigh or enjoy smelling a flower, and you will feel your hand being pushed outwards. This is exactly the way in which you must take a breath when playing the clarinet, although it will often have to be done more quickly. Practise first without the instrument until it becomes automatic. In other words, the *lowest* part of the lungs must be filled with air and you must not be tempted to raise the shoulders and use the upper part in an effort to snatch a quick breath between phrases. *Always* breathe from the very bottom of the lungs. Breathing from the shoulders will cause all the muscles of arms, hands, and fingers to stiffen, and relaxation is one of the first necessities when playing any instrument: if you are tensed-up physically more than is absolutely necessary your playing will be equally tense and uncomfortable to listen to. Quite apart from this, the air-stream when you breathe out again must be controlled from the diaphragm, which will be impossible if only the top portion of the lungs is filled. Whilst playing the clarinet the exhalation of air is obviously much slower than in normal breathing, and every scrap of it must be used to good advantage. Therefore practise inhaling deeply and fairly quickly and exhaling slowly and evenly, at first away from the instrument; then play some long notes (see Chapter I). By listening carefully to yourself you will be able to detect any jerkiness in the passage of air. Feel that the whole process is controlled from the diaphragm, via the abdominal muscles, which support the air column and send it straight through to the bell of the clarinet, the reed and the embouchure acting as sound-producers midway along the route, just as the vocal chords do in singing. It is especially helpful later when playing high notes or a really short staccato to notice this support and even tenseness of the diaphragm. Do not allow any tightening of the throat

muscles. The faster the diaphragm is made to expel the air,
the louder the note; and vice versa. Count a slow four from
the start of the note to the loudest point, and another four
until it dies away again. Remember to make sure that your
body is thoroughly relaxed all the time, except of course for
the vital embouchure and breathing muscles.

How often and when to breathe must be determined by
the phrasing of the music, and of course individual breath
capacities vary. No rules can be laid down; it is entirely
up to the musicianship of the player and it cannot really
be taught. Good breathing punctuates the musical phrases
naturally, just as prose is divided into sentences or poetry
into verses. An abnormally large breath capacity is not
necessarily an advantage unless used with taste; in fact,
there have been famous singers and players who managed
with only one lung. However, there are certain places in
clarinet music where one wishes that it were not necessary
to make any break at all, for example in the opening
twenty-four bars of the slow movement of Schubert's octet,
and the long solo in the second movement of his Unfinished
Symphony. Another difficult passage occurs in the slow
movement of Brahms's second piano concerto:

This can trap the unsuspecting clarinettist, and is well
worth studying.

Inexperienced players often make the mistake of letting
the first breath last too long when they begin a piece just
because they feel fresh. The result is that they feel quite
exhausted for the rest of the piece, which will probably
make the listener feel uncomfortable too. Try to space
your breathing places as evenly as the music allows. If

you find that you still have some breath left at the end of a phrase, get rid of it quickly before breathing in again. If you do not there will be a pocket of air in your lungs which is waste matter and very bad for you. Experience will teach you where to breathe, and playing to an audience or to some friends whenever possible is a help. Very often nervousness affects the breath control; then it is more than ever important to keep relaxed and to breathe deeply and freely, as this will have a soothing influence.

There are often 'danger spots' in certain works where it is best not to take a breath on any account, for example in the slow movement of Brahms's clarinet quintet:

If you breathe between these two phrases you may alter the embouchure slightly, and the note G may refuse to 'speak' at all, or it may suddenly jerk out mezzo-forte, which would be quite the opposite effect from what the composer intended. Try to reorganize the breathing points in the preceding and the following phrase so that you will not need to make a break here. Even in similar places where it *is* absolutely necessary to breathe before a pianissimo phrase, make sure that you hold the instrument quite still in the mouth during the silent beats. A good example of this occurs in Beethoven's Septet:

Try to avoid cutting off the last note of a phrase abruptly in order to take a quick breath for the next. There is *always* time to round it off, or to make the tiniest diminuendo. This is an important part of the art of phrasing, and it can be learnt only by example, not by precept. Listen carefully to a really fine artist on any instrument, and you will notice the little ebbs and flows of tone that go to make up his phrasing. These lie at the very heart of his artistry, and they are not to be explained by performers; only understood. Too many nuances spoil the line of a long phrase; too few make it dull. You must steer your own course between extremes; your teacher can point out some of the more dangerous rocks, but the actual navigation is in your hands.

III

ARTICULATION AND FINGER
EXERCISES

As soon as you are able to play long notes confidently and with a full, rich tone, maintaining the pitch from beginning to end, the next step is to learn to use your tongue. This enables you to articulate, or give a clear and definite beginning to a note, as when pronouncing a word which starts with a consonant. Later the tongue is used to accent notes and for staccato playing (see Chapter VI).

Choose any note, say open G again, and play as for a long note, but on a sustained steady mezzo-forte. While doing this bring the tongue up to touch the tip of the reed gently and withdraw it again, repeating this several times.

You should find that the note reiterates, so:

in the same way that a string player interprets this marking; that is, playing all the notes in one bow, but with a little extra pressure of the bow on each. What actually happens on the clarinet is that the contact of the tongue with the reed momentarily causes it to stop vibrating, giving the articulation. You will find that there are several ways in which this can happen, but the most usual and most natural for most players is for the *tip* of the reed to touch the upper surface of the tongue about $\frac{1}{4}$ to $\frac{1}{2}$ inch away from its tip. You will find more details and a diagram in Chapter VI.

When you have mastered this, try actually beginning a note with the tongue, which should be in position against the reed as soon as you have taken a breath, and withdrawn as you blow, thus giving the note a firm 'edge'. When playing a series of articulated notes the repeated action of the tongue is similar to that used when pronouncing 'Dada-da', one of the first sounds we utter from the cradle. There is no need to use force, because the tongue needs merely to brush the reed to stop it from vibrating. Practise articulating on each note you have learned so far, and you will be well on the way to a natural and easy staccato technique. Every musical phrase must be started in this way, except certain pianissimo ones, where it is best to approach it rather in the same way as the long notes already mentioned. A phrase usually ends with a natural diminuendo, or else with the expiration of breath, not with the tongue (but compare with staccato, Chapter VI).

Assuming that you can now obtain any note downwards from the B♭ above open G, try now to move the fingers whilst actually blowing. Make sure first that they cover the holes correctly, neither stiff and unbending, nor curled up as if clawing at the holes. I have seen both these positions with beginners. The centre of the soft pad of flesh on the underside of the end of each finger must be over the hole. To check this, hold the instrument (without blowing) and press the fingers down abnormally hard; then remove them and look quickly at the impression made by the rings and holes. Some beginners feel discomfort, even cramp, in the right hand after they have been playing for any length of time, which may be due to unsuitable placing of the thumb rest. If the discomfort does not disappear after some perseverance (playing in a relaxed way, of course) a slight adjustment can easily be made one way or the other.

It is generally most difficult to control the lifting of the fingers at first, so here is a technical exercise to help:

If you find it awkward to start at the bottom of the instrument because there are so many more holes to cover, take first the triplet beginning on C and then work downwards. Play each group eight times. Listen carefully to ensure that the tone is of the same quality which you produced

in long notes, and that the movement of fingers is not causing any unsteadiness of the mouthpiece. Make sure also
that each triplet is perfectly even in rhythm. Where there
are alternative fingerings for a note it is a good chance to
become familiar with them. Begin slowly, and as you get
more proficient play the exercise faster. The whole body
should feel relaxed, and the fingers must never stiffen in
an attempt to play rhythmically, nor should they be raised
far from the instrument. It is a good plan when playing
triplets in the right hand to imagine that the left is taking
all the weight of the clarinet, and vice versa: this encour-
ages light and free use of the moving fingers, as if you were
drumming them on a table.

When using the A ('throat note') key it is advisable to
touch only the lowest part of it, and towards the left-hand
side as you look down at it, with the nearest edge of the
left-hand first finger. You will see that it is specially
slanted so that it is easy to reach. In exercise (i) below
all that is needed is a gentle turn, squeeze, or roll of the
finger upwards; do not *lift* it from hole to key. Practise
very slowly and smoothly. Hardly any movement is necessary to uncover the hole and depress the key, although
the wrist may be allowed to turn slightly. The remaining
fingers of the left hand should not be allowed to stray far
from their holes or to huddle together nervously; try
anchoring them by covering the third (C) hole with the
third finger.

In exercise (ii) a similar action is needed for the left thumb,
and in exercise (iii) both first finger and thumb do it
together. Exs. (i) and (ii) are primarily for the Boehm
clarinet, but on all systems the actions just described will
apply to first finger and thumb for exercise (iii).

There is no limit to the finger exercises you can invent.
Here is one for left-hand freedom. Try to avoid any unnecessary movement.

Plenty more technical studies can be found in any tutor or book of technical studies. Exs. (i), (ii), and (iii) above are especially useful as they help in the next technical difficulty, 'crossing the break'.

IV

CROSSING THE BREAK.
HIGHER REGISTER

As any chart will show you, the notes above B♮ (throat note) are played by using again the fingerings of the low register, at the same time opening the speaker key with the left thumb. This takes you as far as the C an octave higher, after which various 'cross fingerings' are used.

Play first the lowest note E on the instrument. While sustaining it open the speaker key and *slightly* tighten the embouchure muscles, thus changing the note to the B a twelfth above.

Playing smoothly over the break

Playing from A to B♮ 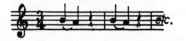 involves bringing into

action simultaneously all the fingers of both hands. It is

similar to the interval , although more diffi-

cult as the speaker key must be opened in addition to the slight adjustment of embouchure. You may find it easier to play downwards over the break first:

Remember the rolling action of the left-hand forefinger (see the last finger exercise in Chapter III). Now try playing upwards.

It is not absolutely necessary to raise all the fingers while playing the note A; the right hand, and even the third finger of the left hand, can remain undisturbed. This does not affect the intonation much on most clarinets, and even if it does, a little preliminary exercise can do no harm so long as you do not make a habit of it. Crossing the break smoothly is one of the major difficulties in clarinet playing, and you will see how important it is never to lift the fingers far from the instrument. When playing a passage which moves forward and backward from open G (or the throat notes) into the higher register it is often possible to leave the right-hand fingers in position throughout, especially if it is a fast passage. You must, of course, be able to play over the break *with* free use of all the fingers, so practise it both ways. This passage from the last movement of Mozart's concerto was doubtless intended to be played an octave lower on a clarinet with extension to low C, but it makes good practice as printed:

Allegro

Some beginners fall into the bad habit of stopping for breath, for instance in a scale, just at the point where it crosses the break, or of tonguing or articulating the difficult note, instead of playing it all as smoothly as possible. Try not to be cowardly: take a breath anywhere else, but not at this place, or you will be a long time in mastering this rather awkward technical point.

As you continue up the scale you will notice that the higher notes are more difficult to control, and it is not so easy to produce a clear, liquid quality. Practise long notes, listening carefully to the intonation; the pitch is likely to waver at first, and sometimes an 'undertone' (or another note) creeps into the pianissimo beginning of a note. This may be caused by one of two things:

(a) The embouchure needs adjusting. Firmer control by tightening of the lip and cheek muscles is needed to support these notes, especially the high A, B, and C, and to give true intonation. 'Forcing the smile' more should help to prevent the note from sounding flat, or the quality from sounding 'wide'. At first the muscles may tire easily, and the fact that there are fewer fingers covering the holes as you go higher may make the instrument feel unsteady in the mouth, but plenty of practice will give you confidence. Experiment by starting the note mezzo-forte and diminishing it to piano, sustaining it for a few seconds, and then making a crescendo. If you can hold a steady pianissimo in this register you will be well on the way to a good control of the embouchure over the whole instrument. Do not be tempted to put more, or less, mouthpiece into the mouth; it may appear to solve the problem at first, but it will alter the tone quality, and obviously would be impossible if you were to meet a passage leaping quickly from high to low notes. Remember to feed the beginning of the note, even if pianissimo, with a strongly supported air supply.

(b) The reed is unsuitable. A reed which is too soft needs more control when playing higher notes, and your embouchure muscles may not be flexible enough yet to give this. Try using a reed cutter (see Appendix II) or a slightly stiffer reed.

Intonation above the high C needs especial care. If you have trouble and are satisfied that your embouchure is not to blame, try using the alternative fingerings which are given in nearly every chart. No two clarinets give the same results in this register; if some of the notes sound flat, for instance, try using one of the right-hand little finger keys: probably the one normally used for Ab/Eb will help. You must find out which fingerings suit your particular instrument the best, checking the intonation by comparing the notes with the same ones an octave lower, as always.

Aim to be able to play any note on the clarinet with

a perfectly controlled crescendo and diminuendo, as was said in the first chapter. Test yourself by taking them in any order, for example a high note followed immediately by the low E; or choose a note and play it in each possible octave. Listen all the time for a beautiful and even quality of sound and good intonation.

Leaps

Composers often ask the clarinettist to play wide intervals up or down in a short space of time, for instance at the opening of Brahms's F minor sonata, or in the first variation in the last movement of Mozart's quintet:

Naturally a certain amount of embouchure flexibility is needed, or else your playing will sound rough and out of tune. It is most helpful to try and hear mentally each note before you sound it, and to imagine the 'feel' of the embouchure you are going to use. Practise at first very slowly, as if it were a heartfelt Adagio, gradually increasing the speed each time until you eventually reach the correct tempo. This, by the way, is a good practice formula for all awkward technical passages. The following exercise is a good preparation, and you can invent many more to help in these kinds of difficulties:

V

SCALES AND ARPEGGIOS

Scales and arpeggios are the foundation of finger technique on any instrument, and you must be very patient in practising them, as they will help you to overcome most of the difficulties of clarinet playing. All classical works, and most post-classical works, are written in the diatonic system of major and minor keys, and so their melody and harmony are based on these principles. A scale is no more than a straight run up or down all the notes of the key the composer has selected and will be using constantly; an arpeggio is generally the notes of one or more chords in that key, played in series. The notes are, as it were, letters; the scales and arpeggios, in whole or in part, are words; and with them the composer writes his music.

As you read this page you do not stop at every word, add up the letters one by one, assemble their sound, and so pronounce the word, which then creates a mental image; your eye takes in the words at high speed, perhaps several at a time, and you understand them. This is because the technique of reading which you learnt in your earliest years has become second nature, which means in fact that your sub-conscious has been trained. You must now train the sub-conscious to read music on the clarinet as efficiently, so that when you see a row of notes going up the stave you do not take each one separately, name it to yourself, think of the fingering, play it, and then start work on the next note; your eye takes it all in, your brain registers 'scale of C major', and by that time your fingers have followed the brain apparently without thought and the passage is played. The ability to recognize scale and arpeggio patterns will also make your transposition more fluent. If you can instantly spot a series of notes as forming a chord of, say, D Major, you can then straightway think of it as E major and play it as easily as if E major were written down. Without this fluency you would have to think out every note, and would so be very much more likely to make mistakes. Of which more later, in Chapter VIII.

It might be held that with the gradual breakdown of the diatonic system in the late nineteenth and early twentieth centuries these arguments are out of date. This is not so: in the first place, there is happily no chance of classical works falling out of the repertory; in the second, you must adapt your scale practice to composers' demands. Practising whole tone scales, for example, will prove useful in the works of Debussy, and it might well be that practising tone-rows would be of value when sight-reading the music of Schönberg and the other twelve-note composers.

The performer must always be ready to adapt his technique to composers' requirements. This point will be returned to in Chapter VII. No one pretends that scale and arpeggio practice is anything but dull, hard work, but its eventual rewards are out of all proportion to the labour involved.

Scales

There are innumerable ways of learning to play scales, and it is best to have a book or tutor containing all the major and minor scales and arpeggios. Your choice may depend on the type of clarinet you play, but make sure that each scale covers the whole range of the instrument, and not just two octaves or so. There are some interesting French, Austrian, and Italian publications, but I favour the forms given in Bärmann's *Daily Studies for the Clarinet* because they are complete and concise and arranged rhythmically in bars.

With a little imagination endless variations in rhythm and articulation can be worked out, and you should play them pianissimo as well as forte, staccato as well as legato, and in as many different rhythms as you can think of. It is best to begin with legato so that you will hear immediately any unevenness; be conscious of each group of four notes and always play very rhythmically. Practise slowly and do not try to force the pace or your scales will sound uncontrolled; speed will come gradually. Play up and down each scale twice to give the fingers a chance to loosen and to encourage your breath control. Eventually you will be able to repeat it several times in one breath.

Here, for example, quoted from Bärmann, is C major, and two possible variants on it:

Interrupted scale:

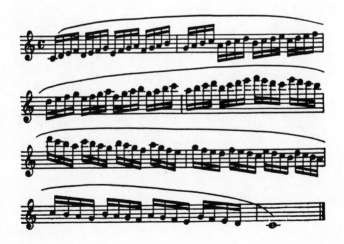

Scale in thirds:

Practise also the relative minor.

Continue in this way with the diatonic scales through all the keys, starting with one sharp in the key signature, then with one flat, then two sharps, two flats, and so on. Never embark on a new key until you are thoroughly familiar with those you have already studied.

Chromatic scales use all the semitones consecutively. Practise throughout the whole range, again in varying rhythms, and make sure that you use the most comfortable fingerings for your particular system of instrument.

Here are some examples of rhythms in which you can practise scales. You can, of course, make up many more of your own.

Arpeggios

Try to play them evenly and with as little adjustment of embouchure as possible; make sure that the fingers are raised and dropped together or else the notes between the intervals will sound.

This figure is a useful one to practise as it takes you over each interval several times. As before, play in all major and minor keys.

Sevenths. So many passages containing dominant and diminished sevenths occur in clarinet music that you should be familiar with them technically.

Dominant seventh:

Diminished sevenths (of which there are only three):

This may seem a bewildering array for daily practice, but of course you can make a selection and work at it for a few days or a week, or choose a key involving some of the technical problems of the piece of music you happen to be studying at the moment. Above all, play always in strict time, and go back constantly over the scales and arpeggios you have already learned. If you have a thorough command over them you can face with confidence a black-looking run of semiquavers when sight-reading. And remember always to be relaxed.

VI

STACCATO

An easy and natural staccato is certainly one of the most important parts of the clarinettist's technical equipment. So many players regard tonguing as a stumbling block, but actually it is not difficult. Confusion usually arises because the teacher cannot see what is going on inside the pupil's mouth and does not bother to find out the exact position of the tongue in relation to the reed and mouthpiece.

Position

As soon as you were able to play long notes you learned to begin a note, or articulate, with the tongue. You will probably have discovered the best position for this at the time. As you are now going to concentrate on playing *short* notes in quick succession it is a good plan to re-examine it carefully. The shortness of the staccato note is governed by the speed with which the tongue returns to the reed to stop it vibrating. The most sensitive part of the reed is its tip, and this is also where the airstream is going to enter. Consequently you will get the best results if the tongue touches the *tip* of the reed.

Now try to find out which part of the tongue will contact the tip of the reed the most easily. While the tongue lies relaxed in the mouth its tip can be felt just behind the bottom teeth. When you put the mouthpiece into your mouth the tongue must merely be pushed slightly forward and upward to make contact with the tip of the reed.

You will probably feel the tip of the reed (and perhaps the tip of the mouthpiece) 'cutting' across your tongue about $\frac{1}{4}$ to $\frac{1}{2}$ inch away from its tip (on the upper and not the under surface, of course). I consider this the normal position for most players, although it is bound to vary according to facial structure, length of tongue, and so on. (See diagram overleaf.)

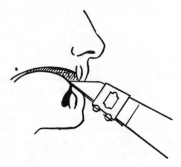

Tip of reed touches tongue

Playing short notes

Begin as in Chapter III with a long sustained open G divided into continuously reiterated sounds by the action of the tongue against the reed, and go on until you feel happy and certain that the tongue is working in the most comfortable way possible.

Now you can begin to aim at short notes for a true staccato, always starting from the long note, and having first taken a really good breath. Instead of merely brushing the reed and then withdrawing, as before, you must now leave your tongue in position against it, and then release it and replace it as quickly as possible. This will give you a short note. When your tongue returns to the reed for the first time you will only have used a fraction of that large breath, and the rest will be waiting in the lungs to be released down the instrument the moment you remove the tongue. Some of the air, but only a very little, may actually escape almost silently down the clarinet, because the tongue should not be pressed so firmly against the reed that it completely closes the aperture. Repeat this quick release-and-return action of the tongue until the whole breath is exhaled. There is nothing more to it.

Notice that it is the force with which the air rushes into the instrument when the tongue is taken away from the reed which gives a clear, crisp, staccato sound, and *not* the striking of the reed with any impetus. It is, in fact, the release of the tongue that produces the attack, not its return. Compare this with a toy balloon. If you pinch the opening tightly between finger and thumb, and then allow the air to escape in bursts by momentarily relaxing them, you will hear a series of puffs. The finger and thumb might be said to correspond to the tongue and reed, and the elasticity of the balloon to that of your diaphragm. The finger and thumb have nothing to do with the suddenness with which the air spurts from the balloon; it is the pressure of the air controlled by the rubber. You will see now the importance of having a large supply of breath ready to be expelled by the diaphragm. In staccato playing you will probably feel an extra tensing of the diaphragm and abdominal muscles, but in my opinion this is perfectly normal and correct, and can help to give more punch and point to your playing. All the other muscles (except of course the embouchure) must be thoroughly relaxed; this is essential if you are to develop any speed with the tongue. Be especially careful not to tighten the throat muscles.

Before going on to discuss speed, here are some warnings against common faults:

(*a*) Do not use the very tip of the tongue against the tip of the reed. This generally involves a certain contraction or contortion of the tongue, and causes unnecessary tightening of the muscles. A minor point is that the splayed tip of the tongue can wear out a good reed rather quickly (see diagram A on the next page).

(*b*) Do not strike the reed too far down, or with too large a part of the tongue's surface. This causes an unpleasant and clumsy sound (see diagram B).

(*c*) Do not tongue without touching the reed at all, either against the lower lip or against the roof of the mouth. Neither can give a really clean start to the note, and in the latter case the tongue has to perform such unnatural gymnastics that it cannot work freely. The less effort it makes the better.

(*d*) Do not expel or 'pump' the breath in short spasms with each note from the diaphragm. It is very exhausting, and of course impossible to do at any speed. It also makes the tongue lazy, because as the air ceases to flow into the instrument after each 'puff' in any case, it is no longer necessary for the tongue to return to the reed to stop the

INCORRECT POSITIONS

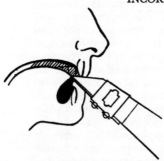

A. Tongue unnaturally stretched so that tip touches reed

B. Tongue too flabby and too low on reed

note. The control of exhalation from the diaphragm must be just as steady as when playing long notes or a legato phrase.

Learning to develop a fast staccato

As you increase the pace the silent 'gap' between the notes is going to become shorter and the tongue must work very quickly. You must therefore never withdraw it far from the reed. As you play faster its action approximates to that of 'du-du-du-du (u as in but) with a gentle d, except of course that the tongue touches the reed instead of the top teeth or the roof of the mouth. It is most useful to practise this away from the clarinet in your spare moments, for instance when out for a walk. Keep relaxed, as always, and your tongue will soon accustom itself to working fast. If you ask some of your friends who have never played a

wind instrument to do this you will find a surprising difference in their speeds. In the same way some clarinettists
find staccato easier than others do. Here are a few examples
of rhythm to practise, either on one note or away from the
instrument:

(useful in the 1st movement
of Beethoven's 7th Symphony)

When you feel satisfied about the position of the tongue
and can work it freely on one note at some speed, try playing scales and studies. If you find that certain notes 'miss'
or sound twice do not always blame your tongue. Perhaps
you are not raising or dropping your fingers absolutely
rhythmically or in co-ordination with the tongue. You
cannot achieve a good staccato in a few days; it needs
patience, but if you are willing to spend ten minutes a day
practising your facility will soon increase. You can test
yourself with a metronome every few days.

Take care that the embouchure is not forgotten, and
that the lip muscles function as in legato playing, the
tongue working quite independently. Very often the tone
quality suffers at first because the lip is slackened in an
effort to let the tongue move freely. This causes notes in
the upper register to sound flat, or an unpleasant 'undertone' to creep into them. Test yourself by playing the
passage legato first to make sure of intonation and quality,
and then, listening carefully, play it again staccato.

Finally, do not be downhearted if the results are at first
not encouraging, or if you hear the flute, oboe, or bassoon
in your orchestra playing a neat staccato with apparently
no trouble at all. Although it is difficult for them too,
I think it is easier than for the clarinet. Perhaps the wedge-
shaped mouthpiece, which forces the jaws apart more,
accounts for this.

Double and triple tonguing

This is not so common on the clarinet as on the flute,
but it is quite possible to cultivate the technique. Articulate

the consonants d-g d-g, or d-g-d d-g-d, as the case may be.

Double tonguing is useful for very rapid staccato passages, as in some Mozart and Rossini orchestral parts. It is also useful for repeated notes, as in the Introduction of Ravel's Septet:

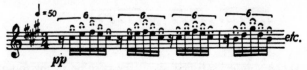

Naturally synchronization of tongue and fingers is more than ever important.

It must be emphasized that double and triple tonguing should not be resorted to because your single tonguing is inefficient. Not only does a good single tongue sound clearer and cleaner, but there are certain critical speeds which are impossible for the double tonguer: they are too fast for his undeveloped single tongue technique, and too slow for double. The result is messy and uneven. By careful practice you can develop a single tongue that is very nearly as fast as a quick double tongue—and you will very seldom come across a passage requiring anything faster than that.

VII

TECHNICAL STUDIES AND
FINGERING DIFFICULTIES

Your practice should include one or more studies from a
tutor or book of studies, as this will help you to use and
combine all the technical points already learned. Most of
them are based on scales and arpeggios, articulated
rhythms, or certain awkward sequences in remote keys. Unfortunately many are very dull musically and are apt to
continue for pages in the same rhythm. Some of the extreme
examples of the breed even have a patterned look, like wall
paper. Try to avoid these; choose those which appeal to you
and play them always as musically as you would any work
in the repertoire, paying attention to the dynamics and
phrasing. Many of Bach's unaccompanied string suites go
well on the clarinet and make wonderful practice.

It would be impossible to mention a complete list here,
but works by Bärmann, Stark, Jettel, Perier, and Uhl are
all good. Especially recommended are Robert Stark's
Practical Staccato School and Alfred Uhl's 48 *Etüden* (Schott).

Some of the most valuable studies are those which you
can make up yourself around tricky passages in clarinet
works. Always find out just where the difficulty lies, and
which note is 'sticking'; do not be content to keep repeating
the passage as it stands in the hope that it will improve if
you go on for long enough. It won't.

As was mentioned in Chapter V, up to and including
the works of Brahms there are very few instances of awkward technical passages which are not based on the various
scales and arpeggios you are studying, but contemporary
works often contain sequences which feel quite foreign to
the fingers. There are some books of studies in the modern
idiom to help, but it is useful to be able to invent your own.

The following examples show you how to set about it,
and they also give some alternative fingerings for use in
special circumstances. There is no need to adhere rigidly

to the fingerings given in your chart; as you advance you will probably discover new ones to help you over difficult passages. Always listen carefully for intonation, though, and be guided by your own taste. Never use a 'faked' fingering for a passage which you could play with the normal one after some practice. Do not be satisfied until you can play the notes backwards as well as forwards, and in any rhythm or tempo, or you will never feel safe with the passage, especially under the strain of performance.

In the following few selected cases I shall try to explain why each passage is difficult and to suggest ways of practising it. Naturally there are endless variations possible, so you must use your own ingenuity and develop the ideas to suit the work you are studying. Always play them in a set rhythm.

(1) Brahms's Quintet, second movement.

Difficulty: cross fingering, involving much raising and lowering of the fingers in a short space of time. Also, as it uses both the higher registers of the clarinet the embouchure must assist and the notes must be coaxed out.

(2) Cadenza from Rimsky-Korsakov's *Coq d'Or*.

Difficulty: continual breaking in the chromatic scale.

(3) Prokofiev's *Peter and the Wolf*.

Difficulty: unusual intervals, with the sequence rising chromatically.

(4) and (5). Here are two awkward passages for you to experiment with: the first is from the second movement of Hindemith's Concerto; and the second occurs at the opening of Elizabeth Maconchy's Concertino. Both contain unusual note sequences and intervals. The former is an excellent left-hand study.

(4)

(5)

(6) Here are two exercises for training the little fingers to find their keys easily.

Use the right-hand little finger throughout (Boehm).

Use the left-hand little finger throughout (Boehm).

The following fingering suggestions apply mainly to the Boehm clarinet, but the general principles and reasons for using them are the same for other systems. In any case, their suitability depends entirely upon the player and the instrument.

Choice of fingerings for B♭/B♮

(7) Opening of Weber's Concerto No. 1 in F minor. Provided that the intonation is satisfactory, use the first finger of the left hand with the second finger of the right (left thumb covering, as usual). In cantabile passages aim to make as little finger movement as possible so as to get a perfect slur.

(8) Mozart's Quintet, second movement; or indeed any passage involving an arpeggio of B♭. Use the first finger of the left hand with the first of the right. For both these examples the correspondence levers joining the two joints of the instrument must be perfectly adjusted or else the pads they operate will not cover well enough to produce the note.

(9) Mozart's Concerto, first movement. Use either the 'long' B♭ fingering as in (8) or the right-hand side key.

(10) Rimsky-Korsakov's *Scheherazade*; also in chromatic scales and in the diatonic scales of F and B♭. Use the left-hand (front) key, which gives neater finger movement and avoids synchronization of the two hands.

(11) Gerald Finzi's Concerto, second movement (written A♯ in the trill). Finger as for G♯, but lift the first finger, left hand. Intonation unsatisfactory, but hardly noticeable at speed, and in any case preferable to an uneven and clumsy movement with keys.

Additional fingerings for higher notes

For E♭ 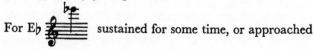 sustained for some time, or approached

by legato leap, try the following fingering:

Cover the second and third finger holes of the left hand, and third finger hole of the right hand. The little finger of the right hand opens the A♭/E♭ key.

But in chromatic passages, or for trilling with D beneath it, take the more usual fingering, covering the second and third holes in the left hand and first in the right (as for D), also depressing the small key between the second and third holes (right hand).

(Left thumb covers hole and opens speaker key for both these examples.)

The piano E 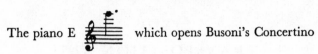 which opens Busoni's Concertino

can be played on some instruments  with the same

fingering as the throat A but with a tighter embouchure. The note can often be coaxed more easily from the instrument, but take care that the intonation is good and that the quality matches the following notes in the phrase.

All the notes in this region can be similarly overblown, but they must be used with discretion, and only in order to serve the phrase musically by avoiding jerky movements.

(12) Brahms's Quintet, third movement. Overblow the initial D from an open G. For similar passages involving C♯ (a semitone lower) overblow F♯.

VIII

TRANSPOSITION AND SIGHT-READING

As you know, the commonest kinds of clarinet are the B♭ and the A. This means in effect that they are built a tone and a minor third respectively below normal pitch, and so the players' parts are written a tone and a minor third *higher* than normal in order to play at the same pitch as

everyone else. For example, if a flute fingers

it is that note which sounds; but if a B♭ clarinet fingers it

the note which sounds is 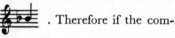 . Therefore if the com-

poser wants his B♭ clarinet to *sound* C, he must write the note a tone higher in order to compensate, that is to say,

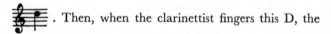 . Then, when the clarinettist fingers this D, the

required C will emerge. The note in the clarinet part has been moved, or, as we say, transposed.

Now this may seem to be going a long way round to get back to where you started. 'Why,' you may ask, 'can clarinets not be built in C?' The answer becomes clear when you hear the C clarinet—a squeaky little instrument, not without its special uses, but having none of the soft, mellow beauty which the larger bore gives the B♭ or A clarinets. Many early clarinets were in C, but it was found that B♭ or A were the two keys in which the instruments could be built most successfully. Beauty of tone is (rightly) preserved at the expense of a certain amount of bother.[1]

The point about having two clarinets is to make it easier. Suppose that the piece you are playing is in E major. To use the B♭ clarinet you would need a part written out in F♯ major, which has a key signature of six sharps. Not only in this unnecessarily tiresome to read, but an effect of the clarinet overblowing at the twelfth is to make the finger technique in extreme keys very much more difficult than it is comparatively on other instruments. If this part were written for A clarinet it would be in G major, i.e. only one sharp. A little thought will show you that pieces in a sharp key require the A clarinet, and pieces in a flat key require the B♭.

So far so good. But supposing, in an orchestral work, the music modulates from a sharp key to a flat one. The composer will then instruct you in your part to change instruments. But often you will come across parts written for C clarinet, and there is no hope for it then but to play on your B♭ or A instrument, transposing the part up a tone or a minor third as you go. This business of mental transposition may sound alarming at first. It needs practice, but it is a knack that can be learnt, and it is an essential part of the clarinettist's technique.

It is a good plan to include some transposition in your daily practice scheme. You must first of all get firmly fixed in your mind the new key signature; then try and play *in the key required* according to the shape of the phrase and the spacing of the intervals. To take a simple example: supposing you had to transpose up a tone the arpeggio of C major. First of all you would decide that the new key was D major, and then, recognizing the shape of the notes in front of you as a common chord, you should trans-

---

[1] Actually clarinets have been built in practically every key from A up to the A♭ clarinet, but the only one of the smaller instruments widely used is the E♭. Its music is written a minor third lower than it will actually sound. There are also instruments pitched lower than the normal A and B♭; the basset horn (in F, sounding a fifth lower than the written note), the alto clarinet (in E♭, sounding a sixth lower than the written note), and the bass clarinet (in B♭, sounding a ninth lower than the written note).

pose it *as a whole* into the arpeggio of D major. Many passages can be treated in this way; try to avoid transposing each note separately up or down the required interval.

C clarinet parts

Most players use the B♭ clarinet and transpose up a tone, especially if the original has flats in the key signature, or perhaps one or two sharps. Accidentals must be watched; very often a flat in the original becomes a natural and a natural becomes a sharp. There is no easy rule of thumb, but experience and musicianship will guide you.

If you read the bass clef easily you will find it best to transpose extreme sharp keys (encountered, for instance, in some Verdi C clarinet parts) on the A clarinet, reading as for the bass clef. Here you must make sure that you are playing in the correct octave (i.e. two octaves higher than if it were in fact the bass clef), and mentally insert the new key signature. Accidentals must be dealt with as they occur.

Prelude to *La Traviata* (Verdi).

Excellent practice for such transposition can be found in the earlier classical sonatas for violin and piano. Most of them suit the range of the clarinet very well, and if you have a partner at the piano it will encourage you not to stop when you stumble over a note, as well as giving you experience of works outside the clarinet repertoire. Even string quartet parts can be used; compared to a stringed instrument the clarinet has such a small field of chamber music (although happily this is being remedied by modern composers), that it is an excellent way of widening your knowledge. The B♭ clarinet can take on viola parts with success. This is done most simply by reading the alto (viola) clef as if it were the bass clef, only one octave higher.

D clarinet parts

As very few people possess a D clarinet, and there are not many instances where it is used, the part must be transposed down a semitone and played on the E♭ clarinet. A well-known example occurs in Strauss's *Till Eulenspiegel*.

Playing A clarinet parts on the B♭

This means transposing down a semitone, and is often convenient when the A clarinet is only wanted for a short time between two longer spells for the B♭. The slow movement of Brahms's first symphony contains a good example; technically it is perhaps even easier, and it does avoid having to pick up a cold instrument. As the clarinettist has two instruments to keep warmed up, it follows that intonation troubles are twice as bad for him as for other woodwind players, but facility in this kind of transposition will help.

Very often composers do not allow sufficient time for the player to change instruments, and then also it is necessary. Find a suitably long rest in your part, either before or after the change is indicated, and change clarinets there, transposing the intervening bars. This often happens between two numbers of an opera or a suite, for instance between the Introduction and the Allegro Vivo of Borodin's Polovtsian Dances from *Prince Igor*. Change well in advance, even omitting some of the *tutti* if necessary in order to be ready for the important solo which follows on the B♭ clarinet.

When transposing an A part down a semitone most players mentally substitute the new key signature, usually in terms of flats. Thus D major becomes D♭ major, and so on. Remember that in doing this the sharps in the original key will become naturals; and that the flats will become double flats.

When playing B♭ parts on the A, which is less common, this entire process is, of course, reversed.

Sight-reading

As in transposition, plenty of practice is the only way to get confidence and facility. If possible play with another person so that you will get a musical idea of the whole and not stop over details. Always look well ahead for any changes of time or key signature, and make sure about the tempo and dynamics before you begin by mentally singing or hearing the first phrase. Concentrate on getting the rhythm right: a few wrong notes will soon be forgotten even if they are noticed, but if you get the time wrong, even for a moment, you will falter and the chances are that the music will come to a standstill. Each time you practise finish by reading something new. There are some excellent books of selected orchestral passages for this purpose.

As you progress in your studies you will find yourself called upon to do more and more sight-reading, in orchestral and chamber work, or trying over new works with composers. It is one of the greatest tests of musicianship to be able to give a first-class impression of the musical idea and mood of a piece at sight, and it calls for every ounce of that equipment which we call clarinet technique.

IX

THE CLARINET IN TWENTIETH-CENTURY MUSIC

by Alan Hacker

The twentieth century encompasses a far wider stylistic range of music than has ever been known before. Composers may have little in common, and, moreover, their own individual development may have involved fundamental changes in style—Schoenberg, Stravinsky, and Stockhausen provide three examples of this. Tonality is no longer always a prime consideration: attack, dynamics, variations in tone have become more important articulations in the writing and performance of music.

It is these areas that the modern clarinettist must develop, alongside the earlier tonal and chromatic traditions and disciplines. But he or she must realize that the contemporary way of extremes and split notes, though perhaps complex and forbidding at first sight, is really based on a deeper feeling for the essence of the clarinet and on a perceptive musical and technical understanding of different styles— not just recognizing the difference between the Vienna and Czech Philharmonics, but knowing about Greek and Turkish playing, and how to sound like a clarinettist on a 1930s dance band record.

Attack

The beginning of a note caused by the vibration of a reed does not necessarily reflect the aggressive implication of the title. Notes that begin from nothing (as in Birtwistle's *Linoi*) can be produced more effectively without using the tongue, by gingerly giving more and more pressure from the diaphragm until the reed vibrates. When starting like this it is important to keep the lips relaxed, to allow the reed to vibrate as soon as enough breath pressure has been provided. It is usually necessary to compensate for sharpness, at such a low dynamic extreme, by closing or partially closing lower holes or keys, gradually opening them as the breath pressure is increased.

Another form of attack involves a more rapid push from the diaphragm, again without the tongue, sometimes squeezing and relaxing the lips at the same time. This gives a kind of quick fade-in and sounds musically urgent and unresolved. When the same technique is also applied in reverse at the end of a note, a life-drained quality is produced, as in the last low Es of *Hymnos* by Peter Maxwell Davies.

A violent attack is produced by an even more rapid diaphragm push while taking the tongue away from the reed. A succession of notes played like this sounds mechanical and quite inappropriate for most earlier music, where the line of a phrase should span the silences or spaces between the notes by means of continuous diaphragm support—in this passage from Dvořák's Seventh Symphony, for example:

A mechanical effect, unphrased and unmusical by the standards of earlier music, is often called for in the twentieth century: in Varèse, Stravinsky, and Peter Maxwell Davies, for example. It is sometimes suggested by the sign v, or by not joining the tails of the notes, as in Birtwistle's *Tragoedia*:

Ideally, if the succession of notes is slow enough each note should be articulated with a thrust from the diaphragm. This can be very exhausting, but is worth the effort, since the musical gesture is essentially physical.

Flutter-tonguing is a familiar articulation in twentieth-century music. Two early works in which this appears are Strauss's *Don Quixote* to represent the braying of sheep, and Berg's *Four Pieces* to heighten the dramatic intensity of the first movement, and as a kind of disintegration in the third movement. This is effected by rolling 'rs', the tongue vibrating on the roof of the mouth. This is difficult from top C upwards. For notes above this a substitute is rapid tonguing or double-tonguing or changing fingerings rapidly (alternating the two top Fs, for example)— solutions for players who cannot roll their rs. 'Growling' might also be the answer!—hum or grunt a semitone away from the note and a beat occurs.

Slap-tonguing, also from the jazz world, is caused by making a suction pad with the tongue and the roof of the mouth which is released forcefully at the beginning of the note.

Dynamics

A wide range can usually be obtained more effectively with middle-of-the-road reeds and mouthpiece lays. Hard reeds on curved open lays produce a fine *ff* but can sound dull in *pp* and strained in *mp* and can cause a sore lip. Closer longer lays can be clearer and more resonant at low levels but have less impact in *ff*, though the sound is possibly more penetrating. As previously mentioned, a correction has to be made to flatten very quiet notes; the opposite can be done to sharpen *ff* notes by opening adjacent lower keys. This kind of technique is very useful in dynamically wide ranging repeated notes, as at the beginning of Peter Maxwell Davies' *Eight Songs for a Mad King*.

Dynamics are often of fundamental importance in twentieth-century music. If Birtwistle's *Linoi* was played without due regard to dynamics, the piece would hardly exist. And in the first movement of the solo pieces of Stravinsky the music depends on the penultimate bar being played slightly more loudly (and faster).

Tone shading and split notes

This depends on the ability of the player and instrument to vary the harmonic content of a note. Certain reeds, mouthpieces, and instruments give more harmonics, so a greater range of colour is possible as there are more harmonics to filter out. A longer parallel bore will produce more harmonics, but perhaps in a mixture that does not appeal to the player. Whoever the player, or whatever the instrument, however, maximum harmonics are produced by the strongest breath pressure, and vice versa. As an example, play low C at *mf* but with the lowest possible breath pressure and the slackest embouchure. Now increase the breath pressure without changing the embouchure, and the tone will grow in harmonic content. Eventually a harmonic, a G or a flat E perhaps, will dominate,

and the original C will disappear; this is like overblowing the baroque oboe, flute, and tin whistle to the second register. Play the actual pitches also so that you have the intervals in your mind. Now attempt to bring back C while retaining an overblown pitch. In order to make a sound on low C which has even less harmonic content than you started with, find another fingering! Finger low F sharp, and open the C sharp key—this is a very flat C sharp or a poorly vented C natural. Now increase pressure as before, and E natural and B flat will appear.

This triad is not really a clarinet chord, but the dividing of one note into three clearly audible pitches, the fundamental and two harmonics; the other fingering not only gives a different basic tone quality but of course different harmonics.

Much more detailed information can be found in Bruno Bartolozzi's *New Sounds for Woodwind* (O.U.P.) and in William O. Smith's *Variants for Clarinet* (U.E.). But the most important thing is to understand the principle, because different equipment will produce different pitches and because many works do not specify or necessarily require exact pitches, the point being simply colouring (Boulez's *Domaines*), emotional distortion (*Miss Donnithorne's Maggot* and *Eight Songs for a Mad King* by Peter Maxwell Davies), punctuation (Birtwistle's *Verses for Ensembles*), or imitation of ring-modulation (Peter Maxwell Davies' *Steadman Caters*).

APPENDIX I

PURCHASE AND CARE OF INSTRUMENT

When buying a clarinet make sure to get expert advice, particularly of course if you are a beginner and know nothing of the instrument. If you are already a player you may want to better your equipment, so here are a few hints on what to look for when buying an instrument. An expert should always be called in before the final choice is made; and no matter how expert you are yourself, a colleague's opinion is always of interest. You do not have to follow his advice.

The B♭ clarinet is the best to start with as on the whole it is used more often than the A, especially in the technically easier pieces. If you are interested in playing in a military band or a dance band it is essential. Later you may be able to find an A clarinet to match, or alternatively you can sell the B♭ and buy a pair.

Whether you decide on a new or a second-hand instrument:

(a) It must be low pitch. An old high pitch clarinet which has been converted by lengthening the tube will not do, whatever anyone tells you.

(b) The material must be good black ebony. Clarinets have been made from different kinds of metal, ivory, porcelain, ebonite, and plastic, but matured Mozambique ebony gives the best sound. The drawback about it is that it is sensitive to violent changes of atmosphere, and in extreme climates other materials have been found more satisfactory. Some instruments have bakelite bells and barrels, but the main body should be of wood, and there must naturally be no cracks. The most likely places for these to occur are round the holes, near the joints or near the pillars supporting rods and keys; always look carefully at these when considering an instrument for buying. The inside of the bore should be smooth.

(c) The keys should not be so soft that they can be easily bent with the hand. Springs and pads are not so important, as they can be replaced at comparatively low cost.

(d) The intonation should be good, and this is perhaps the most vital point of all. This means that the notes must be in tune with each other, in addition to the note A conforming to the standard pitch of 440 at a room temperature of 60°. Unfortunately there is no such thing as a wind instrument which is perfectly in tune. Also, a good clarinet may be thrown out of tune by using a mouthpiece of the wrong internal measurements; remember this when examining a second-hand one. Even two mouthpieces made by the same firm may give different intonation on any one instrument as the tonal chambers or internal measurements may not be similar, but some of the better ones have a serial number on each part so that no mistakes can be made. Mouthpieces are relatively quite cheap, and it is quite possible to have one specially made to suit the intonation of a good instrument.

System of fingering

Most eminent players now use the Boehm clarinet, although it is unfortunately the more expensive. Simple system clarinets can often be seen in shop windows for only a few pounds, but they are not always low pitched. The alternatives, with values related to the best quality, are:

A or B♭, first quality, new
A or B♭, first quality, second-hand, half the price of the above
B♭, cheapest quality, new, one quarter the price
  (There is not always an A to match)
B♭, cheapest quality, second-hand, one-fifth the price

It is best to buy either a very expensive or a very cheap instrument; the former always has a market value if you ever want to make a change or give up playing, and with a cheap one your loss is negligible and more than compensated for by the hours of pleasure it has given. If someone offers to make you a present of a clarinet, accept

gratefully! You can always check up on its points afterwards.

When buying a pair, see that they are matched, made
by the same firm, and that the same mouthpiece fits and
suits each. Obviously this is important for orchestral playing when one has to change instruments frequently.

Parts and care of clarinet

Starting from the base of the instrument the parts are:
Bell
Lower joint
Upper joint
Barrel, or socket
Mouthpiece, to which is attached the reed by a ligature. This is usually of metal; German and Austrian players
bind their reeds on with cord, but it is interesting to note
that in these countries, where musical traditions are adhered
to so strongly, the metal ligature is now beginning to be
used.

Assembly. All joints are lapped with cork or cord, which
should be kept slightly greased. The parts should be assem-
bled with a twisting movement. If the joint is too stiff,
grease it with a little Vaseline; if it is too loose, swell the
cork by wetting or greasing it and then passing a match
lightly underneath it. On some models particular care
must be taken to see that the lever projecting from the
upper joint falls exactly over its counterpart on the lower
joint. This ensures that the finger holes are in alignment
and that the ring and pad mechanism receives correct and
uniform pressure. In warm weather, or if the pitch of the
clarinet rises a little after a prolonged spell of playing or
in an overheated concert hall, the barrel can be unscrewed
so that there is a slight gap between the outsides of it and
the upper joint. This counteracts the sharpness, and it is
therefore important that this joint should be kept in good
condition and correctly greased.

Always leave the metal cap on the mouthpiece to protect
the reed while you are assembling the instrument. Do not
take it off until the last possible moment. The side with the
reed attached must of course be in line with the back of

the instrument, above the left-hand thumb hole and key and the right-hand thumb rest. Always replace the cap even if you only put the instrument down for a few minutes.

Springs and pads. The springs must be just strong enough to hold the keys down, ensuring that the hole is airtight, but not so strong that they impair the agility of the fingers. Keep them oiled, and also oil the key rods between the pillars, but see that none touches the pads. A light oil marketed under the name of '3-in-1' is suitable for this purpose. Skin pads are best, and they should be watched for any suspicion of leaking or becoming water-logged, and renewed when necessary. Otherwise an embarrassing gurgle may ruin a beautiful phrase! If you do suffer this misfortune, blow sharply across and into the hole. A piece of cigarette paper placed under the key will then absorb any surplus moisture. If you have recurrent trouble with water in the same hole, consult your teacher.

Bore. From time to time a light dampening of the bore with linseed oil is advisable. Put cigarette papers under the pads to protect them, and do it with a special cloth. Most important of all is the regular cleaning of the bore each time after playing, even if you have only been playing for a very short time. This is best done with a pull-through, similar to that used for rifles in the Army. It removes condensation, making the bore smooth and polished, and this in turn helps to improve the tone. It is, by the way, probably not true to say that a clarinet mellows and matures with age to the extent that a violin does, for instance.

The player must gradually adapt himself to his instrument and learn to get the best from it, always handling it carefully and keeping it in perfect working order. It is a good plan to have it completely overhauled every year or so.

APPENDIX II

CHOICE OF MOUTHPIECE AND REED

The mouthpiece is usually made of ebonite, and as the reed (which is flat) is placed against the opening, obviously the face of it must fall or curve away in order to leave an aperture through which the breath can enter and start the reed vibrating. There are many possibilities of the exact degree of slope, and different angles suit different players and types of playing. Research has shown remarkably little variation between the lays, or slopes, of eminent players' mouthpieces. A correct lay gives the resistance necessary to control the air flow and produce a real pianissimo or fortissimo. Consult a craftsman if you wish to check or re-lay your mouthpiece; he may have the measurements of some well-known players, which will help you to decide which is the best for you.

A close or medium lay tends to give a more refined, firmer sound with control of tone gradations; an open lay is more suitable for glissandos and vibrato. Of course, there are endless variations between the two. It depends a great deal on the player and the reed used, and here expert advice is invaluable. Once you have found a comfortable lay persevere with it; so many players do themselves more harm than good by constantly altering their lays, and consequently their embouchures, to say nothing of the time they waste.

Reeds

Plastic or cane can be used to make reeds, but so far the plastic reed has not been found satisfactory to the experienced musician playing chamber music, or for solo or orchestral work. This is unfortunate as it has the advantage of great lasting powers. Possibly in the future a composition reed will be produced which will give the good tone quality of cane and the long life of plastic, and then the clarinettist using a cane reed will be as rare as the violinist using a gut E string is now.

Unfortunately a good cane reed can only be selected by playing on it, and not by looking at it, so it is best to buy twenty-five or so at a time, or at the very least three or four. Then you can select the best for performing and perhaps use the others for practice. If a reed is transparent for some way down from the tip, thin and very flexible, it will be a soft reed; and a hard reed has the opposite features. For an untrained lip it is best to start with a fairly soft reed, but remember that if it is too soft the tone will be thin and weak. If it is too hard unnecessary effort will be needed to produce a note, which will be a harsh sound accompanied by air and a fluffy noise. It usually takes a little time before the reed feels settled on the mouthpiece, and its character can alter with use. The action of the tongue can make it thinner and softer, although sometimes moisture hardens it. The same reed can feel and sound quite different on two different lays; usually a reed which suits a wide lay is too soft on a close lay, and vice versa. Make sure that you buy reeds which are correct for your particular mouthpiece, and not necessarily those recommended by a friend, who may use quite a different lay.

The reed should be a good golden colour, with a fine even grain; a slightly greenish reed denotes immature cane. The best cane is grown in France, and reeds manufactured there are usually the finest. Especially good are those made by Vandoren. If you should happen to be in Paris try to visit Vandoren's to replenish your stock. The shop is in the rue Lepic, Paris (Montmartre). Or you can persuade friends to bring some back for you. Some players make their own, but so far not to the extent in this country that oboe players do. Reeds are graded into boxes of soft, medium, and hard, but one can, and usually does, find a surprising selection of all grades in any one box, regardless of its label. The quality of cane has deteriorated since the war because many of the bamboo plantations were cut down and the sticks used as camouflage for tanks and guns. Afterwards the cane had to be planted afresh, and there is good reason for believing that it is often cut and made into reeds nowadays before it is sufficiently seasoned.

Great care must be taken when affixing the reed to see that it sits absolutely straight and centrally on the face of the mouthpiece. It should be held with the thumb and first finger of the left hand and adjusted with the thumb

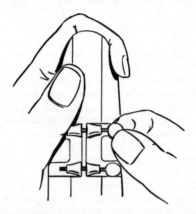

of the right hand. The normal position leaves a fraction of the mouthpiece showing above the reed, little more than a black line when looking at the instrument held vertically. If the reed is inclined to be too soft it should be placed a little higher so as to give more resistance; if it is too hard, place it a little lower. These adjustments must be only slight.

When a reed is too thin, and gives insufficient resistance, as often happens when it has been played for some time, a reed cutter can be used to clip a little off the tip and so stiffen it. If it has too much resistance it can be scraped carefully with a very sharp knife or razor blade on the shaded part of the reed (as illustrated).

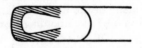

Sometimes, after a reed has been played for some time it seems to lose its resilience, and feels unresponsive to the tongue. You can help matters by inserting, very carefully, a piece of stiff paper or card, about the thickness of a postcard, between the reed and the mouthpiece. Gently ease it downwards so that it separates the reed from the mouthpiece a little. Remove it carefully. (This recommendation applies mostly to players using a fairly close-lay mouthpiece.)

These devices cannot be relied upon to improve a reed. It is primarily the quality of cane which produces a fine sound, and without a first-class reed it is impossible to give a beautiful and sensitive performance.

PREPARING FOR EXAMINATIONS AND PUBLIC PERFORMANCE

by John Davies

Preparing for an examination and for a public performance present virtually the same problems. In either case
therefore you should consider the following: preparation
and presentation of programme; care and condition of
instrument; intonation; stance; general deportment; and
theatre of performance.

Concerning preparation and presentation of programme,
it hardly needs stating that technical proficiency, control of
legato and articulation, ability to phrase musically, and an
understanding of the style and character of the works to be
performed are fundamental requirements. They should be
coupled with adequate rehearsal with your pianist or
ensemble. Your choice and construction of programme is
equally important. The works chosen should be suited to the
technical and interpretative capability of the player,
bearing in mind the need to offer a contrast in musical
style which incorporates both technical brilliance and
cantabile playing. You should also endeavour to build a
varied programme, including classical, romantic, and
contemporary works.

The necessity for your instrument to be in the best
possible mechanical order is obvious. Rods and springs
should be well oiled, correspondence perfectly adjusted,
pads seated down with correct venting, and no grease or
fluff in the laterally bored holes. The bore itself should be
kept highly polished and the corks well greased.

The player will need to ensure that the integral tuning of
the instrument has been as well maintained as possible. It
is also vital to be adequately 'warmed up' before performance and to have an easily manœuvrable barrel, thus

facilitating the adjustments which are made necessary by fluctuations of temperature.

A good stance enables the performer to maintain a position of balance involving the least muscular strain whilst playing. Deportment when entering and leaving an examination room or platform is also important. This should be executed in a calm and unhurried manner and the bow should be made gracefully.

In performance it is necessary to show your colleagues and audience that it is your intention to commence. This should be no more than a momentary 'freezing' of the body followed (for your colleagues' benefit) by some physical indication such as a nod of the head. It is very important to remain still during rest bars, and a reasonable pause at the end of movements is also tasteful. The phrase 'theatre of performance' really means that your behaviour and deportment should bear some relation to the character and style of the works performed.

On no account should the player show concern or display any other reactions to problems that may occur during performance.

The above advice will help the performer to play with some structure and authority. But it must be remembered that it is essential for performers to give something of themselves—the degree of personal involvement being the vital factor.

The Diploma examinations of the recognized musical institutions do not have a rigid format. Nevertheless there are certain guide-lines which are usually followed. The examinee will be called upon to give a performance of the set works with piano accompaniment, as well as a technical study, scales, sight-reading, and transposition. The candidate will also have to work a paper with questions related specifically to wind-playing. Finally, questions will be asked viva voce—this may take the form of a demonstration lesson given to an imaginary pupil. The following is a guide to the sort of questions that the candidate may be asked:

1. How to assemble and care for your instrument.
2. How to produce the first note, taking into consideration:

(a) The formation of the embouchure and instructions as to its control
(b) the finger, hand, and arm positions
(c) the angle of the clarinet in relation to the body.

3. Articulation in its varying forms.
4. Breathing—here a demonstration and explanation of diaphragmatic breathing will be necessary.
5. Development of tone, and methods of improving the quality.
6. Methods of developing technique.
7. An explanation of phrasing.
8. How to practise, and the daily quota necessary for pupils at varying stages of development.
9. Alternative fingerings and trills.
10. Questions appertaining to the clarinet as a transposing instrument.
11. Naming the registers of the clarinet and describing their tonal characteristics.
12. Explanation of the Harmonic Series as related to the clarinet.
13. Suggested format of a lesson.
14. Knowledge of repertoire, studies, and methods.
15. History and development of the instrument.
16. Famous players who have inspired composers to write for the instrument.
17. The aural and physical requirements of students intending to study this particular instrument.
18. The motivation of students.
19. Advice on the purchase of an instrument.
20. Choice and care of reeds.
21. Material available for group playing in schools.
22. Questions concerning works performed in the examination, which require a knowledge of their composers and an understanding of their structure, interpretation, style, tempo, phrasing, and dynamic levels.

This covers most of the topics that are likely to crop up.

APPENDIX IV

A LIST OF MUSIC FOR THE CLARINET

compiled by Georgina Dobrée

The following catalogue does not pretend to be an exhaustive list of repertoire. Readers are further referred to:

Flute Repertoire Catalogue by Frans Vester (MR)
The Clarinet by Oskar Kroll (Batsford)
The Clarinet by F. Geoffrey Rendall (Williams & Norgate)
Clarinet by Jack Brymer (Macdonald and Janes)

and individual publishers' catalogues.

The list is arranged as follows:

Clarinet studies
Solo clarinet
Clarinet duets
Three and more clarinets
Concertos for clarinet
Concertos for more than one solo instrument, including clarinet
Clarinet (etc.) and piano
Clarinet(s) and strings
Clarinet(s) and strings with piano
Clarinet and other wind instruments, excluding wind quintets
Wind quintets
Wind and piano
Wind and strings
Wind, with or without strings, and other instruments not included in other categories
Clarinet(s), with or without other instruments, and tape
Voice(s) with not more than 4 instruments, including clarinet(s)

ABBREVIATIONS OF PUBLISHERS' NAMES

ACA	American Composers Alliance
AMP	Associated Music Publishers
Bä.	Bärenreiter
B & H	Boosey & Hawkes
B & B	Bote & Bock

Br.	Breitkopf & Härtel
BCMA	British & Continental Music Agencies
Broude-A	Alexander Broude
CMC	Canadian Music Centre
CBDM	Centre Belge du Documentation Musicale
CHF	Ceský Hudebni Fond, Prague
CFE	Composers Facsimile Edition (ACA)
Cundy-B	Cundy-Bettoney
DFM	Dan Fog Musikforlag
DSS	Drustvo Slovenskih Skladateljev, Ljubljana
ECA	Edición Culturales Argentinas
EMB	Edition Musica Budapest
Elkan-V	Elkan-Vogel
Hin.	Hinrichsen
Hof.	Hofmeister
IEM	Instituto de Extensión Musical, Santiago
IMC	International Music Catalogue
MCA	MCA Music, N.Y.
McG & M	McGinnis & Marx
MPI	Music Press Inc.
MR	Musica Rara, London
OUP	Oxford University Press
PWM	Polskie Wydawnictwo Muzyczne, Warsaw
SUDM	Samfundettil Udgivelse af Dansk Musik, Copenhagen
SPAM	Society for the Publication of American Music
S & B	Stainer & Bell
STA	STA Private Edition, California, U.S.
SANU	Srpska Akademija Nauka i Umetnosti, Belgrade
UE	Universal Edition
VEB	VEB Deutscher Verlag für Musik

ABBREVIATIONS FOR INSTRUMENTATION

fl.	flute	hn.	horn
picc.	piccolo flute	bn.	bassoon
ob.	oboe	cb.	contra bassoon
eh.	English horn (cor anglais)	tr.	trumpet
		trom.	trombone
cl.	clarinet	vn.	violin
bhn.	basset horn	va.	viola
bcl.	bass clarinet	vc.	cello

db.	double bass	str. 3	string trio (vn., va., vc.)
pf.	piano		
hp.	harp	str. 4tet	string quartet (2vn., va., vc.)
timp.	timpani		
perc.	percussion	str. 5tet	string quintet (str. 4tet + db.)
sax.	saxophone	wind 5tet	wind quintet (fl., ob., cl., hn., bn.)
bar.	baritone		
sop.	soprano		

CLARINET STUDIES FOR THE INTERMEDIATE TO ADVANCED STUDENT

BAERMANN, C.: Complete Celebrated Method (*Fischer*)

BERNARDS, B.: Rhythmical Studies for the Clarinet (*Zimmermann*)

BLANCOU, V.: 40 Etudes (*Leduc*)

BOZZA, E.: 12 Etudes (*Leduc*)

CAVALLINI, E.: 30 Caprices (*IMC; Leduc*); 12 Etudes (*Leduc*)

ELIA, A. D': 12 Technical Studies—Full Boehm (*Ricordi*)

GABUCCI, A.: 60 Divertimenti (*Ricordi*); 10 Fantasie (*Ricordi*); 20 Studies of Medium Difficulty (*Ricordi*); 10 Etudes de Grande Difficulté (*Leduc*)

GAMBARO, J. B.: 10 Caprices, Op. 9 (*IMC*); 12 Caprices, Op. 18 (*IMC: Ricordi*); 22 Progressive Studies (*Ricordi*)

GAMBARO, V.: 21 Caprices (*Ricordi*)

GIAMPIERI, A.: incl. 12 Modern Studies (*Ricordi*)

JEANJEAN, P.: incl. 16 Etudes Modernes (*Leduc*)

JETTEL, R.: Klarinettenschule (*Doblinger*); The Accomplished Clarinettist (*Weinberger*)

KELL, R.: incl. 17 Staccato Studies (*IMC*)

KLOSE, H.: Méthode Complète (2 vols.) (*Leduc*)

KROEPSCH, F.: 416 Studies (*Schmidt: IMC*)

LANCELOT, J.: incl. 15 Etudes (*Transatlantiques*)

LANGENUS, G.: Complete Method (*Fischer*)

LANGEY, O.: Practical Tutor (*B & H*)

PERIER, A.: incl. 30 Etudes (*Leduc*)

ROSE, C.: 26 Etudes (*Leduc*); 40 Studies (*IMC*)

RUEFF, J.: 15 Studies (*Leduc*)

SIGEL, A.: The 20th Century Clarinetist (*Belwin Mills*)

STARK, R.: 24 Studies in all tonalities (*IMC*); 24 Virtuosity Studies
　　Op. 51 (*IMC*)
THURSTON, F. & FRANK, A.: The Clarinet: A Comprehensive
　　Method (*B & H*)
UHL, A.: 48 Studies for Clarinet (*Schott*)

SOLO CLARINET

AITKEN, H.: Suite (*Elkan-Vogel*)
APOSTEL, H. E.: Sonatine, Op. 19, no. 2 (*UE*)
ARMA, P.: Petite Suite (*Lemoine*)
ARNOLD, M.: Fantasy, Op. 87 (*Faber*)
BABIN, V.: Divertissement Aspenois (*Augener*)
BÁLLIF, C.: Solfeggietto no. 5 (*Transatlantiques*)
BARTOLOZZI, B.: The Hollow Man—for any woodwind
BAVICCHI, J.: Sonata no. 2 (*OUP*)
BENTZON, J.: Theme and Variations, Op. 14 (*Hansen*)
BERGAMO, P.: Concerto Abbreviato, Op. 10 (comp. *Belgrade*)
BIRTWISTLE, H.: 4 Interludes from a Tragedy
BOIS, R. DU: Three Pieces for Clarinet (*Donemus*)
BOULEZ, P.: Domaines—version for solo cl. (*U.E.*)
BRINDLE, R. SMITH: Sikel (*New Wind Music*)
CAGE, J.: Sonata (*Peters*)
CAMILLERI, C.: Three Visions for an Imaginary Dancer (*Fairfield/
　　Novello*)
CHAGRIN, F.: Improvisation and Toccatina (*Augener*)
CHESLOCK, L.: Descant (*OUP*)
COLE, B.: Triptych—The Odes of Gemini (*MS*)
CONSTANT, M.: For Clarinet (*Salabert*)
DEÁK, C.: Sonatina (*Nordisk/Chester*)
DONIZETTI, G.: Study (*Peters*)
DUBOIS, P.-M.: Sonata Breve (*Leduc*)
ESCHER, R.: Sonata (*Donemus*)
GELBRUN, A.: Partita (*Israel Mus. Inst.*)
GIPPS, R.: Prelude (*Joseph Williams*)
GOEHR, A.: Paraphrase on the dramatic madrigal—'Il Combat-
　　timento di Tancredi e Clorinda' by Claudio Monteverdi
　　Op. 28 (*Schott*)
HARTZELL, E.: Monologue I—Sonatina (*Doblinger*)
HEIDER, W.: Inventio 11 (*Ahn & Simrock*)
HOVHANESS, A.: Lament (*Peters*)
IOANNIDIS, Y.: Versi (*Gerig*)
JACOB, G.: Five Pieces (*OUP*)
JETTEL, R.: 5 Grotesken (*Eulenberg*)

JENNI, D.: Musica della Primavera (*AMP*)
JOLIVET, A.: Asceses (*Billaudot*)
KAGEL, M.: Atem (UE)
KARG-ELERT, S.: Sonata Op. 110 (*Zimmermann*)
KOECHLIN, C.: Monodies Op. 215 (*MS.*)
KRENEK, E.: Monologue (*Rongwen*)
LADERMAN, E.: Serenade (*Peters*)
LANG, I.: Monodia (*Ed. Mus. Budapest*)
LAPORTE, A.: Reflections (*Chester*)
LEHMANN, H. U.: Mosaik (*MS.*)
LEWIS, R. H.: Monophonies no. 3 (*Doblinger*)
LUTYENS, E.: Tre Op. 94 (*UE*)
MAGNANI, A.: 3 Sonates (*Evette*)
MARTINO, D.: incl. 'B, A, B, B, IT, T' (written for clarinet in B♭, at concert pitch) with extensions (*Ione*); Strata *bcl.* (*Ione*)
MAYER, J.: Raga Music (*Lengnick*)
OLAH, T.: Sonate (*Salabert*)
OSBORNE, W.: Rhapsody (*Hin.*)
OSORIO-SWABB, Reine: Sonatine 1946 (*Donemus*)
PERLE, G.: 3 Sonatas (*Presser*)
PFEIFFER, H.: Prelude, Scherzo and Fugue (*Lienau: McG & M*)
POUSSEUR, H.: Madrigal 1 (*UE*)
RIVIER, J.: Les Trois 'S' (*Transatlantiques*)
ROSENBERG, H.: Sonata (*Suecia*)
ROZSA, M.: Sonatine Op. 27 (*Rongwen*)
RUGGIERO, G.: incl. 20 Divertimenti (*Sikorski*)
SMITH, W. O.: Five Pieces (*UE*): Variants (*UE*)
STOCKHAUSEN, K.: incl. Solo (*UE*)
STRAVINSKY, I.: Trois Pièces (*Chester*)
SUTERMEISTER, H.: Capriccio (*Schott*)
TAILLEFERRE, G.: Sonate (*Peters*)
TOMASI, H.: Sonatine Attique (*Leduc*)
TUTHILL, B.: Two Snacks for Alonesome Clarinet (*Southern*)
WELLESZ, E.: Suite Op. 74 (*Rongwen*)
WHITTENBERG, C.: 3 Pieces Op. 29 (*McG & M*)
WILKINSON, M.: Adagio and Variations (*MS.*)

CLARINET DUETS

BACH, C. P. E.: 2 Duets (*Presser*)
BACH, W. F.: Duo no. 1 (*Broekmans/UE*)
BENNETT, R. R.: Crosstalk (*UE*)
BORGHI, L.: Divertimento no. 2 (*Presser*)
BUTTERWORTH, A.: incl. Three Dialogues (*Peters*)

BUTTERWORTH, N.: Divertimento (*Peters*)
CAVALLINI, E.: Two Grand Duets (*Cundy-B*)
CHAGRIN, F.: 6 Duets (*Novello*)
CRUFT, A.: Duo Op. 67 (*Peters*)
CRUSELL, B.: Three Progressive Duets (*Hin.*); Duo no. 1 and Duo no. 2 (*Sikorski*)
DEVIENNE, F.: Duos Op. 69 nos. 1 & 2, Op. 69, no. 3 (*Schott*)
DONIZETTI, G.: Sonate (*Eulenberg*)
ELTON, A.: Short Sonata (*Chester*)
FRANK, A.: Suite (*OUP*)
GEBAUER, F. R.: 6 Duos Concertants Op. 2 (*Sikorski*)
HARVEY, J.: Studies (*Novello*)
HARVEY, P.: Satirical Suite (*Schott*)
HESS, W.: 5 Duos (*Hin.*)
KOECHLIN, C.: Idylle (*Chant du Monde*)
KREUTZER, K.: Duo in C (*Sikorski*)
LEFÈVRE, X.: 6 Petits Duos Faciles (*Costallat*)
LEWIN, G.: Two of a Kind (*B & H*)
MCCABE, J.: Bagatelles (*Novello*)
MANNINO, F.: Les Feuilles d'Automne Op. 72 (*Curci*)
MIRANDOLLE, L.: 3 Duos (*Leduc*)
MOZART, W. A.: 12 Duets (orig. 2 bhn./2 hn.) (*OUP*)
PLEYEL, I.: Duos Op. 14, nos. 1–3 (*Marks*)
POULENC, F.: Sonata (B♭ & A) (*Chester*)
PRANZER, J.: Duo Concertant and Duo no. 3 (*Transatlantiques*)
ROE, C.: Three Bagatelles (*New Wind Music*)
SAYGUN, A. A.: Sezisler Op. 4 (*Southern*)
STADLER, A.: Duo in F (*Sikorski*)

THREE AND MORE CLARINETS

ABSIL, J.: Quatuor E♭, 2 B♭ & bcl.
ARMA, P.: Sept Transparances 4 cl. (*Lemoine*)
ARRIEU, C.: 5 Mouvements E♭, 2 B♭ & bcl. (*Billaudot*)
BOUFFIL, J.: Trios Op. 7 nos. 1–3 & Op. 8 (*Cundy-B*)
BOZZA, E.: Sonatine E♭, 2 B♭ & bcl. (or wind 4tet) (*Leduc*)
CAILLIET, L.: Fantaisie 4 cl. (1st doubles E♭) (*Leblanc*)
CARTER, E.: Canonic Suite 4 cl. (*AMP*)
COOKE, A.: Suite for 3 clarinets (*OUP*)
CRANMER, P.: Prelude and Fugue E♭, B♭ & bcl. (*MS.*)
DESPORTES, Y.: French Suite 4 cl. (*Southern*)
DONATO, A.: Three Pieces 3 cl. (*UE*)
FERNEYHOUGH, B.: Sonatina 3 cl. & bcl. (*Hin.*)

GABRIELSKY, W.: Grand Quartet Op. 43/1 4 cl. or 3 cl. & bcl. (*Southern*)

HARDING, K.: Quartet 3 cl. & bcl. (*MS.*)

HARVEY, P.: Four Easy Trios (*Schott*); Quartet 3 cl. & bcl. (*Schott*)

HASHAGEN, K.: Perpetuum mobile 4 cl.

HOLLOWAY, I.: Die Kunst der Klarinette 3 cl. & bcl. (*Schirmer*)

HOVHANESS, A.: Divertimento 3 cl. & bcl. (or wind 4tet) (*Peters*)

HUMMEL, J. F.: Trio (*Simrock*)

JACOBSON, I. D.: Three Caprices 3 cl. (*Mills*)

JELINEK, H.: Divertimento Op. 15/8 E♭, B♭, bhn., bcl. (*UE*)

KOLASINSKI, J.: Little Suite 3 cl. (*PWM*)

MICHALSKY, D.: Divertimento 2 cl. & bcl. (*Avant*)

MIHALOVICI, M.: Sonata E♭, A & bcl. (*Salabert*)

MIRANDOLLE, L.: Quartet 2 cl., alto cl. & bcl. (*MS.*)

MOZART, W. A.: 4 Divertimenti (K. 439b) 3 cl. (orig. 3 bhn.) (*OUP*); Adagio K.411 2 cl. & 3 bhn. (Br.)

NORTH, R.: Ballet Suite 2 cl. & cl./bcl. (*MS.*)

NUDERA, A.: 2 Divertimenti 3 cl./3 bhn. (Hof.)

OWEN, H.: Chamber Music 4 cl. (Avant)

PAUER, J.: Divertimento 3 cl. (*Bä.*)

PIKET, F.: Legend and Jollity 3 cl. (*Omega*); Reflection and Caprice 4 cl. (*Omega*)

QUINET, M.: Suite 4 cl. (*CBDM*)

REINER, K.: Music for 4 cl. (*CHF*)

ROWLEY, Alec: Nocturne 4 cl. (*Augener*)

SEMLER-COLLERY, J.: Quartetto (*Eschig*); Pièce Récréative 5 cl. (*Eschig*)

STARK, R.: Sonata in G minor 2 cl. & bhn. (*Hin.*); Serenade 2 cl., bhn. & bcl. (*Schmidt*)

TCHEREPNIN, A.: Trio (*Belaieff*)

TOMASI, H.: Trois Divertissements 4 cl. (*Leduc*)

TOWNSEND, D.: Ballet Suite 3 cl. (*Hin.*)

TUTHILL, B.: Intermezzo Op. 1/2 2 cl. & bhn. (*Fischer*)

UHL, A.: Divertimento 3 cl. & bcl. (*Schott*)

VERRALL, J.: Serenade 3 cl., alto cl. & bcl. (*UE*)

WATERSON, J.: Grand Quartet 4 cl. or 3 cl. & bcl. (*Southern*)

WILKINSON, P.: Suite 4 cl. (or wind 4tet) (*Novello*)

CONCERTOS FOR CLARINET

APIVOR, D.: Concertant (*MS.*)

ARNOLD, M.: Concerto (str. orch.); Concerto No. 2 (*Lengnick*)

BECK, C.: Concerto (*Schott*)

BEN-HAIM, P.: Pastorale Variée (*MCA*)

BEREZOWSKY, N.: Concerto Op. 28 (*B & H*)

BERIO, L.: Chemins 2c Bcl.

BOULEZ, P.: Domaines (*UE*)

BRUNS, V.: Concerto (*Hof.*)

BUSH, G.: Rhapsody (str. orch.) (*Elkin*)

BUSONI, F.: Concertino (ch. orch.) (*Br.*)

COOKE, A.: Concerto (str. orch.) (*Novello*)

COPLAND, A.: Concerto (str. orch. & hp.) (*B & H*)

CRUFT, A.: Concertino (str. orch.) (*Jos. Williams*)

CRUSELL, B.: Concerto Op. 5 (*Sikorski*)

DEBUSSY, C.: Première Rhapsodie (*Durand*)

DRAGATAKIS, D.: Chamber Concerto (str. orch.)

ETLER, A.: Concerto (ch. orch.) (*AMP*)

EVANS, P.: Concerto (str. orch.)

FINZI, G.: Concerto (str. orch.) (*B & H*)

FLOTHUIS, M.: incl. Concerto Op. 58 (*Donemus*)

FRANÇAIX, J.: Concerto (*Transatlantiques*)

GARGIULO, T.: Serenata (str. orch., pf., perc.) (*Curci*)

GOTKOVSKY, Ida: Concerto (*Transatlantiques*)

HAMILTON, I.: Concerto Op. 7 (*MS./Schott*)

HEIDER, W.: Strophen (*Peters*)

HINDEMITH, P.: Concerto (A) (*Schott*)

HODDINOTT, A.: Concerto (str. orch.) (*OUP*)

HODGSON, P.: incl. Concerto (str. orch.) (*Hin.*)

HOFFMEISTER, F. A.: Concerto (*Schott*)

HOROVITZ, J.: incl. Concerto Op. 7 (str. orch.) (*Mills*)

JOSEPHS, W.: Concerto (*Novello*)

KEYS, I.: Concerto (str. orch.) (*Novello*)

KOECHLIN, C.: Sonatas Opp. 85 & 86 (ch. orch./pf.) (*Oiseau Lyre*)

KOPPEL, H. D.: Concerto Op. 35 (*SUDM*)

KOZELUH, (J. A.?): Concerto (*Musica Viva, Prague*)

KROMMER, F.: Concerto Op. 36 (*Artia/B & H*)

LARSSON, L.-E.: Concertino Op. 45/3 (str. orch.) (*Gehrmans*)

LUCAS, L.: Concerto (*MS./Chester*)

LUTOSLAWSKI, W.: Dance Preludes (*PWM*)

MACONCHY, E.: Concertino (str. orch.) (*MS.*)

MATHIAS, W.: Concerto

MILHAUD, D.: Concerto (*Elkan-V*)

MOLIQUE, B.: Concerto (*Bä.*)

MOLTER, J. M.: Concerto no. 3 arr. B♭ cl. (str. orch. & cont.) (*Schott*); Concertos 1–4 (cl. in D) (*Br.*)

MOZART, W. A.: Concerto K.622 (A) (incl. *Br.: Schott*, for reconstruction of original version for basset-clarinet by Alan Hacker)

MUSGRAVE, T.: Concerto (*Chester*)

NIELSEN, C.: Concerto Op. 57 (*Dania*)

PATTERSON, P. Concerto (*Weinberger*)

PETRIĆ, I.: Concerto (ch. orch.) (*DSS*); Mosaiques (ch. ens.) (*DSS*)

PISTON, W.: Concerto (*AMP*)

PLEYEL, I.: Concerto in C (*MR*); Concerto in B♭ (*Sikorski*)

POKORNY, F.: Concerto in E♭ (*Br.*); Concerto in B♭ (*Br.*)

RAJIĆIĆ, S.: Concerto no. 2 (str. orch. pf., perc) (*SANU*)

RAWSTHORNE, A.: Concerto (str. orch.) (*OUP*)

RIMSKY-KORSAKOV, N.: Concerto with military band (*B & H*)

RIOTTE, P. J.: Concerto Op. 24 (*Sikorski*)

RISTIĆ, M.: Concerto

RIVIER, J.: Concerto (*Transatlantiques*)

ROSETTI (ROESLER), F. A.: Concerto in E♭ (*Rubank*); Concerto in E♭ (*Kneusslin*)

ROSSINI, G.: Introduction, Theme and Variations (*Sikorski*); Variations for cl. and small orch. (*Zanibon*)

SCHUBERT, M.: Concerto 1971 (*VEB*)

SEIBER, M.: Concertino (str. orch.) (*Schott*)

SHAW, A.: Concerto (*Mills*)

SIEGMEISTER, E.: Concerto (*Fox*)

SPOHR, L.: Concerto no. 1, Op. 26 (*Peters: IMC*); Concerto no. 2, Op. 57 (*Peters: Cunáy-B: IMC*); Concerto no. 3 (*Br.: IMC*); Concerto no. 4 (A) (*Br.: IMC*)

STAMITZ, C.: Concerto no. 1 (in F) (trans. B♭ cl.) (*Schott*); Concerto no. 3 (in B♭) (*Peters*); Concerto in B♭ (no. 10) (*Sikorski*); Concerto in E♭ (Darmstädter) (*Hof.*); Concerto in E♭ (no. 11) (*Schirmer*); Concerto in E♭ (*Sikorski*)

(N.B. All these concertos are different works.)

STAMITZ, J.: Concerto (str. orch.) (*Leeds: Schott*)

STANFORD, C. V.: Concerto Op. 80 (*MS./Stainer & Bell: J. B. Cramer*)

STEVENS, H.: Concerto (str. orch.)

STILES, F.: Concerto

STRAVINSKY, I.: Ebony Concerto with military band (*Chappell*)

SZERVÁNSKY, E.: Concerto (*EMB*)

TCHAIKOWSKY, B.: Concerto (*Sikorski*)

TOMASI, H.: Concerto (*Leduc*)

TUTHILL, B.: Concerto

UHL, A.: Konzertante Sinfonie (*UE*)

VEALE, J.: Concerto (A) (*OUP*)

VINTER, G.: Concertino (*B & H*)

WANHAL (VANHALL), J.: Concerto (*B & H*)

WEBER, C. M. von: Concertino Op. 26; Concerto no. 1, Op. 73; Concerto no. 2, Op. 74 (incl. *B & H: Br.*)

WEINER, L.: Ballade Op. 8 (*Zenemukiakó Vállalat*)
WHETTAM, G.: Serenade no. 1 (*De Wolfe*); Concerto, Op. 40 (*Mills*)
WILDGANS, F.: incl. 2nd Concerto (*Doblinger*)

CONCERTOS FOR MORE THAN ONE SOLO INSTRUMENT, INCLUDING CLARINET

ANDRÉ, P.: Concertino 2 cl. (*Deplaix*)
BERIO, L.: Concertino vn. & cl. (hp., celeste, str.) (*UE*)
BLACHER, B.: Konzertstück wind 5tet (str. orch.) (*B & B*)
BRUCH, M.: Concerto cl. & va. (*Eichmann: The Viola Society*)
DEVIENNE, F.: Symphonie Concertante Op. 25 2 cl. (*MR*)
DURKÓ, Z.: Una rapsodia ungherese 2 cl.
HINDEMITH, P.: Quadruple Concerto fl., eh., cl., bn. (*Schott*)
HOFFMEISTER, F. A.: Concerto in E♭ 2 cl. (*MR*)
HOLBROOKE, J.: Quadruple Concerto fl., ob., cl., bn. (*De Wolfe*)
KROMMER, F.: Concerto Op. 35 2 cl. (*MR*)
MARTELLI, H.: Concertino Op. 85 ob., cl., hn., bn. (str. orch.) (*Ricordi*); Concerto cl. & bn. (*Moeck*)
MOZART, W. A.: Sinfonia Concertante ob., cl., hn., bn. (*Br.*)
NYSTEDT, K.: Concertino cl. & eh. Op. 29 (str. orch.)
PHILLIPS, BURRILL: Triple Concerto cl., va. & pf.
STAMITZ, C.: Concerto in B♭ 2 cl. (*Peters*); Concerto in B♭ cl. & bn. (*Sikorski*)
STARER, R.: Concerto a tre cl., tr. & trom. (str. orch.)
STRAUSS, R.: Duet-Concertino cl. & bn. (str. orch. & hp.) (*B & H*)
TELEMANN, G. P.: Concerto 2 cl./2 chalumeaux (*MR*)
WINTER, P. VON: Concertino cl. & vc. (*Sikorski*)

CLARINET (or basset horn, bass clarinet, etc., if indicated) AND PIANO

ALESSANDRO, R. D': Sonata giocosa (*Sidemton*)
ALWYN, W.: Sonata (*B & H*)
ANDRIEU, F.: incl. Divertissement (*Billaudot*)
ARMA, P.: Divertimento no. 6 (*Lemoine*)
ARNELL, R.: Eight Pieces (*Hin.*)
ARNOLD, M.: Sonatina (*Lengnick*)
AURIC, G.: Imaginées 3 (*Salabert*)
BABIN, V.: Hillandale Waltzes (*B & H*)
BAERMANN, H. (formerly attrib. Wagner): Adagio (*Br.*)
BAIRD, T.: 2 Caprices (*PWM/UE*)
BANKS, D.: Prologue, Night Piece & Blues for Two (*Schott*)

BARAT, J.: incl. Fantasie Romantique (*Leduc*); Solo de Concours (*Leduc*)

BAX, A.: Sonata (*Chappell*)

BEN-HAIM, P.: Pastorale Variée (*Israel Mus. Publ.*); Songs without Words (*Israel Mus. Publ.*)

BENJAMIN, A.: Le Tombeau de Ravel (*B & H*)

BENTZON, J.: Kammerconcert no. 3, Op. 39 (*Hansen*)

BERG, A.: Four Pieces Op. 5 (*UE*)

BERNARD, J.: Sonatina (*OUP*)

BERNSTEIN, L.: Sonata (*Witmark*)

BIRTWISTLE, H.: Verses (*UE*); Linoi 1 (*UE*)

BJELINSKI, B.: Sonata (*Gerig*)

BLYTON, C.: Scherzo (*New Wind Music*)

BOIELDIEU, F. A.: Sonate (*Simrock*)

BOISDEFFRE, R. DE: incl. Sonata Op. 12 (*Hamelle*)

BOWEN, Y.: Sonata (*MS.*)

BOZZA, E.: incl. Bucolique (*Leduc*)

BRAHMS, J.: Sonatas Op. 120 nos. 1 & 2 (incl. *Wiener Urtext Ed.*)

BROWNE, P.: A Truro Maggot (*B & H*)

BRUNS, V.: Sonate Op. 22 (*Pro Musica, Leipzig*); Vier Stücke Op. 44 (*Br.*)

BURGMULLER, N.: Duo Op. 15 (*Schott*)

BURT, F.: Duo Op. 7 (*UE*)

BUSONI, F.: Elegie (*Br.*)

BUSSER, H.: incl. Cantegril Op. 72 (*Leduc*)

BUTTERWORTH, N.: Pastorale (*New Wind Music*)

BYRNE, A.: Two Pieces (*Hin.*); Suite (*Hin.*)

CAPLET, A.: Improvisations (*Durand*)

CAMILLERI, C.: incl. Piccola Suita (*Waterloo*)

CARDEW, PHIL: incl. The Lazy Faun (*New Wind Music*); Scherzo (*B & H*)

CARTER, E.: Pastoral (*Presser*)

CAVALLINI, E.: incl. Adagio and Tarantelle (*Cundy-B*); Elégie (*Ricordi*)

CHAGRIN, F.: incl. Sarabande (*Lengnick*)

COOKE, A.: Sonata (*Novello*); Alla Marcia (*OUP*)

COWELL, H.: 3 Ostinati with Chorale (*MPI*); 6 Casual Developments (*Merion*)

CRUFT, A.: Impromptu Op. 22 (*Jos. Williams*)

DALBY, M.: Pindar is Dead (*Novello*)

DANZI, F.: Sonata in B♭ (*Simrock*); Sonata for bhn. Op. 62 (*Hof.*)

DAVIES, P. MAXWELL: Hymnos (*B & H*)

DEBUSSY, C.: 1ère Rhapsodie (*Durand: Peters*); Petite Pièce (*Durand: Peters*)

DEVIENNE, F.: Première Sonate (*Transatlantiques*); Deuxième Sonate (*Transatlantiques*)
DUBOIS, P. M.: incl. Sonatina (*Leduc*)
DUKAS, P.: Alla Gitana (*Leduc*)
DUNHILL, T.: Phantasy Suite Op. 91 (*B & H*)
EDMUNDS, C.: incl. Gay Hornpipe (*Schott*)
ETLER, A.: Sonata (*AMP*); Sonata no. 2 (*Broude-A*)
FERGUSON, H.: Four Short Pieces (*B & H*)
FINZI, G.: Five Bagatelles (*B & H*)
FULTON, N.: Three Movements (*Augener*)
GADE, N.: Phantasy Pieces (*Hansen*)
GÁL, H.: Sonata Op. 84 (*Hin.*)
GALLOIS MONTBRUN, R.: Concertstück (*Leduc*); Six Pièces Musicales d'Etude (*Leduc*)
GARANT, S.: Asymétries
GIBBS, C. ARMSTRONG: Three Pieces (*OUP*)
GOEHR, A.: Fantasias Op. 3 (A) (*Schott*)
GOW, D.: Three Miniatures (*Augener*)
GROVLEZ, G.: Lamento et Tarantelle (*Leduc*); Sarabande et Allegro (*Leduc*)
HAMILTON, I.: Three Nocturnes (A) (*Schott*); Sonata (*Schott*)
HARVEY, J.: Transformations of 'Love bade me welcome' (*Novello*)
HEAD, M.: Echo Valley (*B & H*)
HEIDER, W.: Dialog (*Peters*)
HERVIG, R.: Sonata no. 2 (*MS.*)
HINDEMITH, P.: Sonata (*Schott*)
HODDINOTT, A.: Sonata Op. 50 (*OUP*)
HOFFMEISTER, F. A.: Sonata (A) (*MR: Schott*)
HOLBROOKE, J.: Andante and Presto (*B & H*); 4 Mezzotints Op. 55/8 (*Cary*); Nocturne Phrine (*Modern Mus. Lib.*)
HOLD, TREVOR: The Blue Firedrake
HONEGGER, A.: Sonatine (A) (*Salabert*)
HOROVITZ, J.: Two Majorcan Pieces (*Mills*)
HOWELLS, H.: Sonata (*B & H*)
HURLESTONE, W.: Four Characteristic Pieces (*Cary*)
IBERT, J.: Aria (A) (*Leduc*)
IRELAND, J.: Fantasy-Sonata (*B & H*)
JACOB, G.: Sonatina (A) (*Novello*)
JETTEL, R.: incl. Sonata (*Hof.*)
KALABIS, V.: Sonata Op. 30 (*Panton*)
KARG-ELERT, S.: Sonata Op. 139b (A) (*Zimmermann*)
KARKOFF, M.: Nocturne Op. 81
KELLY, B.: Two Concert Pieces (*Novello*)
KENDELL, I.: incl. Episode (*Chester*)

KENINS, T.: Divertimento (*B & H*)

KISIELEWSKI, S.: Sonata (*PWM*)

KOECHLIN, C.: Sonatas Opp. 85 & 86 (*Oiseau Lyre*)

KOHS, E.: Sonata (*Merrymount*)

KOPPEL, H.: Variations Op. 72 (*Leduc*)

KORNAUTH, E.: Sonata Op. 3 (*Doblinger*); Sonata Op. 5 (*Zimmermann*)

KOTOŃSKI, W.: 6 Miniatures

KRENEK, E.: Suite (*Schott*)

KUBIK, G.: Sonatina (1959)

LADMIRAULT, P.: Sonate (*Leduc*)

LANGFORD, A.: Scherzetto (*Arcadia*)

LEFEBVRE, C.: Fantasie Caprice (*Leduc*)

LEFÈVRE, X.: Sonatas—Op. 12/1 (*OUP*); Op. 12/3 (*Richli*). From the Méthode, Sonatas no. 1 (*Schott*); no. 5 (*Richli*); no. 7 (*Ouvrières*)

LEGLEY, V.: Sonata Op. 40/3 (*CBDM*)

LEVY, E. I.: Sonata

LOGOTHETIS, A.: Desmotropie

LLOYD, C.: Suite in the Olden Style (*B & H*); Duo Concertante (*Novello*)

LUENING, O.: Fantasia brevis (*New Music*)

LUTOSLAWSKI, W.: Dance Preludes (*PWM/Chester*)

LUTYENS, E.: Valediction Op. 28 (A) (*Mills*); Five Little Pieces (A) (*Schott*)

MCCABE, J.: incl. Three Pieces (*Novello*)

MARTINON, J.: Sonatine (*Billaudot*)

MARTINU, B.: Sonatine (*Leduc*)

MATHIAS, W.: Sonata (*Mills*)

MENDELSSOHN, F.: Sonata (*Schirmer*)

MESSAGER, A.: Solo de Concours (*Leduc*)

MIHALOVICI, M.: Sonata (*Heugel*); Dialogues (*Heugel*)

MILFORD, R.: Lyrical Movement (*OUP*)

MILHAUD, D.: Sonatine (*Durand*); Duo Concertant (*Heugel*)

MIRANDOLLE, L.: incl. Sonata (*Leduc*); Sonatina (*Leduc*)

MOESCHINGER, A.: Sonatina Op. 65 (*B & H*)

MURRILL, H.: Prelude, Cadenza and Fugue (*OUP*)

NICULESCU, S.: Inventions (*Salabert*)

NORTH, R.: Sonata (*Chester*)

ORNSTEIN, L.: Nocturne (*Elkan-V*)

PASCAL, C.: Six Pieces Variées (*Durand*)

PATTERSON, P.: Conversations (*Weinberger*)

PERLE, G.: Sonata quasi una fantasia (*Presser*)

PERT, M.: Sonata (*Weinberger*); Luminos bhn. (*Weinberger*)

PIERNÉ, G.: incl. Canzonetta (*Leduc*)
PIGGOT, P.: Fantasia (*Leduc*)
PISK, P.: Sonata (*CFE*)
PITFIELD, T.: incl. Conversations (*Leeds*); Conversation Piece (*OUP*)
POBJOY, V.: Four Pieces (*Schott*)
POULENC, F.: Sonata (*Chester*)
PURSER, J.: Dances of Ilion
RABAUD, H.: Solo de Concours (*Leduc*)
RAFTER, L.: Five Satires (A) (*Bosworth*)
RAINIER, P.: Suite (A) (*Schott*)
REIZENSTEIN, F.: Arabesques Op. 47
REGER, M.: Sonatas—Op. 49/1 (*UE*); Op. 49/2 (A) (*UE*); Op. 107 (*B & B*)
REINECKE, C.: Sonata Op. 167 (A) (*IMC*)
RHEINBERGER, J.: Sonata Op. 105a (*Schott*)
RICHARDSON, A.: incl. Roundelay (*OUP*)
RICHARDSON, N.: Sonatina (*B & H*)
RIDOUT, A.: Sonatina (*Schott*)
RIES, F.: Sonata Op. 29 (*Schott*); Sonate Sentimentale Op. 169 (*MR: Bä*)
ROCHBERG, G.: Dialogues (*Presser*)
ROHWER, J.: Sonata (*Möseler*)
ROUSSEL, A.: Aria (*Leduc*)
RUDOLPH, ARCHDUKE: Sonata (A) (*MR*)
RUEFF, J.: Concertino (*Leduc*)
SAINT-SAËNS, C.: Sonata Op. 167 (*Durand*)
SCHMITT, F.: Andantino (*Leduc*)
SCHOENBERG, A.: Sonata (from Wind 5tet arr. Greissle) (*UE*)
SCHUMANN, R.: Fantasiestücke Op. 73 (A or B♭) (*Schirmer*)
SEARLE, H.: Suite Op. 32 (*Schott*); Cat Variations (A) (*Faber*)
SEIBER, M.: Andantino Pastorale (*Schott*)
SEMLER-COLLERY, J.: incl. Cantabile et Allegro (*Billaudot*); Fantasie et Danse en forme de Gigue (*Leduc*)
SHAW, C.: Sonata (*Novello*)
SMITH-MASTERS, A.: Zoo Walks (*Anvil*)
SOWERBY, L.: Sonata (*SPAM*)
SPINNER, L.: Suite Op. 10 (*B & H*)
SPOHR, L.: incl. Fantasie and Variations Op. 81 (*Schmidt*); Andante and Variations Op. 34 (*Schmidt*)
STANFORD, C.: incl. Sonata Op. 129 (*Stainer & Bell*)
STEEL, C.: Sonatina Op. 11 (*Novello*)
STEVENS, H.: Suite (*Hin.*)
STEVENSON, R.: Nocturne—Homage to John Field

STOKER, R.: Sonatina (*Leeds*)

SWAIN, F.: incl. The Willow Tree (*British & Continental*)

SZALOWSKI, A.: Sonatina (*Omega*)

TANEIEV, S.: incl. Sonate (*Benjamin*)

TCHAIKOWSKY, A.: Sonata Op. 1 (*Weinberger*)

TEMPLETON, A.: Pocket-sized Sonata 1 (*Leeds*); Pocket-sized Sonata 2 (*Shawnee*)

TOMASI, H.: incl. Introduction et Danse (*Leduc*)

TOVEY, D. F.: Sonata Op. 16 (*Schott*)

TUTHILL, B.: Fantasy Sonata Op. 3 (*Fischer*)

VAUGHAN WILLIAMS, R.: Six Studies in English Folk Song (*Stainer & Bell*)

VICTORY, G.: Suite Rustique (*Leduc*)

VINTER, G.: Song and Dance (*Weinberger*)

VLAD, R.: Improvisazione su di una melodia (*Ricordi*)

VLADIGUEROV, P.: Trois Aquarelles Op. 37/1 (A) (*Sofia*)

VLIJMEN, J. VAN: Dialogue (*Donemus*)

WAGNER, R.: Adagio (see BAERMANN, H.)

WALKER, E.: Romance Op. 9 (*Jos. Williams*)

WALKER, J.: Sonatina (*Schirmer*)

WANHAL (VANHALL), J.: Sonata in Bb (*McG & M*); Sonata in Bb (*orig. C*) (*MR*); Sonata in Eb (*Schott*)

WEBBER, L.: Theme and Variations (*Francis, Day & Hunter*)

WEBER, C. M. VON: Grand Duo Concertant Op. 47 (*IMC: Schirmer*); Theme and Variations Op. 33 (*Schirmer: IMC: Lienau*); also versions with piano reductions of Introduction, Theme and Variations (*IMC: B & B*); Grand Quintet Op. 34 (*Lienau*)

WEINER, L.: Ballade Op. 8 (*Rozsavölgyi*); Peregi Verbunk Op. 40 (*Zenemukiakó Vállalat*)

WELLESZ, E.: Two Pieces Op. 34 (A) (*UE*)

WHETTAM, G.: Sonatina (*Leeds*)

WILDGANS, F.: incl. Sonatina (*Doblinger*)

WILLIAMSON, M.: Pas de Deux (*Weinberger*)

WILSON, T.: Sonatina (*Schott*)

WORDSWORTH, W.: Prelude and Scherzo (*Lengnick*)

CLARINET(S) AND STRINGS

ANDRIESSEN, J.: Quartetto Buffo cl. & str. 3 (*Donemus*)

BACH, J. C.: 3 Quartets Op. 8 cl. & str. 3 (*Cundy-B*)

BAERMANN, H. (formerly attrib. WAGNER): Adagio cl. & str. 5tet (*Br.*)

BENJAMIN, A.: Quintet cl. & str. 4tet (*B&H*)

BENTZON, J.: Intermezzo Op. 24 cl. & vn. (*Hansen*)
BEREZOWSKY, N.: Duo Op. 15 cl. & va. (*Leeds*)
BERG, G.: Duo cl. & vn. (*DFM*)
BLATT, F.: Theme and Variations cl. & str. 4tet (*Simrock*)
BLISS, A.: Quintet cl. (A) & str. 4tet (*Novello*)
BLUMER, T.: Trio Op. 55 cl., vn., vc. (*Simrock*)
BOATWRIGHT, H.: Quartet cl. & str. 3 (*OUP*)
BOWEN, Y.: Fantasy Quintet bcl. & str. 4tet (*De Wolfe*)
BRAHMS, J.: Quintet Op. 115 cl. (A) & str. 4tet (incl. *Peters: IMC*)
BUSCH, A.: Hausmusik Op. 26, nos. 1 & 2 cl. & vn. (*Br.*); Deutsche
    Tänze Op. 26/3 cl., vn., vc. (*Br.*)
BUSH, G.: Rhapsody cl. & str. 4tet (*Elkin*)
CAZDEN, N.: Quartet cl. & str. 3
COLERIDGE-TAYLOR, S.: Quintet cl. & str. 4tet (*MR*)
CONNOLLY, J.: Triad Op. 19 cl., vn., vc. (*Novello*)
COOKE, A.: Quintet cl. & str. 4tet (*OUP*)
CRUSELL, B.: Quartets cl. & str. 3 Opp. 2, 4 & 7 (*Kneusslin*)
CUSTER, A.: Permutations cl., vn., vc. (*Joshua/Novello*)
DAHL, I.: Concerto a Tre cl., vn., vc. (*Arrow*)
DAVID, J. N.: Sonata Op. 23/4 cl. & va. (*Br.*)
DAVID, T. C.: Quintet cl., str. 3 & db. (*Doblinger*)
DIAMOND, D.: Quintet cl., 2 va., 2 vc. (*Southern*)
DIJK, J. VAN: Trio cl., va., vc. (*Donemus*)
DRUCE, D.: Jugalbundi cl. & va.
EDER, H.: Quartet cl. & str. 3 (*Br.*); Quintet cl. & str. 4tet (*Br.*)
EKLUND, H.: Liten Serenad cl., vn., db. (*Nordiska*)
ENGEL, J.: Suite cl. & str. 5tet (*UE*)
FELDMAN, M.: Two Pieces cl. & str. 4tet (*Peters*)
FRANKEL, B.: Quintet Op. 28 cl. & str. 4tet (*Chester*)
FROMM-MICHAELS, I.: Musica Larga cl. & str. 4tet (*Sikorski*)
FUCHS, R.: Quintet Op. 102 cl. & str. 4tet (*Robitschek*)
GÁL, H.: Serenade cl., vn., vc. (*MS.*)
GEBAUER, E.: Duo concertant Op. 16/3 cl. & vn. (*MR*)
GIPPS, R.: Rhapsody cl. & str. 4tet (*MS.*)
GOLDBERG, T.: Quintet Op. 7 cl. & str. 4tet (*B & B*)
GUNDRY, I.: Duo cl. & vc. (*Hin.*)
HAMILTON, I.: Quintet Op. 2 cl. & str. 4tet (*Schott*); Quintet
    (no. 2) cl. & str. 4tet; Serenata cl. & vn. (*Presser*)
HARRISON, P.: Quintet cl. & str. 4tet (*MS.*)
HEIDRICH, M.: Trio Op. 33 cl., vn., va. (*Schmidt*)
HEMEL, O. VAN: Quintet cl. & str. 4tet (*Donemus*)
HÉROLD, S.: Serenade cl., vn., va. (*Schmidt*)
HINDEMITH, P.: Variations cl. & str. 3 (*Schott*); 2 Stücke cl. & vn.
    (*Schott*); Quintet Op. 30 cl. (B♭ & E♭) & str. 4tet (*Schott*)

HODDINOTT, A.: Nocturnes and Cadenzas Op. 53 cl., vn., vc. (*OUP*); Quartet cl. & str. 3

HOELLER, K.: Quintet Op. 46 cl. & str. 4tet (*Müller*)

HOESSLIN, F. VON: Quintet cl. (A) & str. 4tet (*Simrock*)

HOFFMEISTER, F. A.: Quartet cl. & str. 3 (*Doblinger*)

HOLBROOKE, J.: Quintet Op. 27 cl. & str. 4tet (*Blenheim*)

HOWELLS, H.: Rhapsodic Quintet Op. 31 cl. & str. 4tet (*S & B*)

HUMMEL, J. N.: Quartet cl. & str. 3 (*MR*)

HUSA, K.: Evocations de Slovaquie cl., va., vc. (*Schott*)

INGENHOVEN, J.: Sonatina cl. & vn. (*Tischer & Jagenberg*)

JACOB, G.: Miniature Suite cl. & va. (*MR*); Quintet cl. & str. 4tet (*Novello*)

JETTEL, R.: Trio cl., vn., va. (*Doblinger*)

JUON, P.: Divertimento Op. 34 cl. & 2 va. (*Schlesinger*)

KELTERBORN, R.: Lyrische Kammermusik cl., vn., va. (*UE*)

KORNAUTH, E.: Quintet Op. 33 cl. & str. 4tet (*Doblinger*)

KREHL, S.: Quintet Op. 19, cl. (A) & str. 4tet (*Simrock*)

KREIN, A. A.: Esquisses hébraïques Op. 12, nos. 1 & 2 cl. & str. 4tet (*Jurgensen*)

KROMMER, F.: 13 Pieces Op. 47 2 cl. & va. (*Kneusslin*); Quartets Op. 69, Op. 82 (A), Op. 83 cl. & str. 3 (*MR*); Quintet Op. 95 cl., vn., va. (vn.), va., vc. (*MR*)

LANDRÉ, G.: 4 Miniaturen cl. & str. 4tet (*Donemus*)

LEERINK, H.: Trio cl., va., vc. (*Donemus*); Sonata Op. 19 cl. & vc. (*Donemus*)

LEFANU, N.: Quintet cl. & str. 4tet (*Novello*)

LINN, R.: Duo cl. & vc.

LOCKWOOD, N.: Quintet cl. & str. 4tet

LOKSHIN, A.: Quintet cl. & str. 4tet

MACONCHY, E.: Quintet cl. & str. 4tet (*OUP*); Sonata cl. & va.

MARTEAU, H.: Quintet Op. 13 cl. & str. 4tet (*Alsbach*)

MARTINO, D.: Quartet cl. & str. 3 (*Ione*)

MARTINU, B.: Sérénade 2 cl. (C) & str. 3 (*Eschig*)

MOORE, D.: Quintet cl. & str. 4tet

MOZART, W. A.: Quintet K.581 cl. (A) & str. 4tet (incl. *Bä.: IMC*)

MÜLLER, S. W.: Divertimento Op. 13 cl. & str. 4tet (*Br.*)

NERUDA, F.: Musikalische Märchen Op. 31 cl., va., vc. (*Hansen*)

NEUKOMM, S. R. VON: Quintet Op. 8 cl. & str. 4tet (*Simrock*)

NOWAK, L.: Trio cl., vn., vc. (*ACA*)

PICHL, W.: 3 Quartets Op. 16 cl. & str. 3 (*Longman*)

PRAAG, H. VAN: Prelude, Intermezzo and Scherzo cl. & vc. (*Donemus*)

RAPHAEL, G.: Serenade Op. 4 cl. & str. 4tet (*Simrock*); Duo Op. 47/6 cl. & vn. (*Müller*)

RAWSTHORNE, A.: Quartet cl. & str. 3 (*OUP*)

REGER, M.: Quintet Op. 146 cl. (A) & str. 4tet (*Peters*)

REICHA, A.: Quintet Op. 89 cl. & str. 4tet (*MR*); Quintet Op. 107 cl. & str. 4tet (*Zanibon*); Sextet 2 cl. & str. 4tet (*McG & M*)

REIZENSTEIN, F.: Theme, Variations and Fugue Op. 2 cl. & str. 4tet ((*Lengnick*)

ROMBERG, A. J.: Quintet Op. 57 cl., vn., 2 va., vc. (*Peters*)

ROSEN, J.: Sonata cl. & vc.

SALIERI, G.: Adagio con variazioni cl. & str. 4tet (*Sikorski*)

SCHUBERT, K.: Quintet cl. & str. 4tet

SEIBER, M.: Divertimento cl. & str. 4tet (orig. version of Concertino) (*MS.*)

SHAFFER, J.: Quintet cl. & str. 4tet

SMITH, W. O.: Suite cl. & vn. (*OUP*)

SOMERVELL, A.: Quintet cl. & str. 4tet

SPOHR, L.: Andante & Variations (arr. mov't Op. 34) cl. & str. 4tet (*Schmidt*); Fantasie and Variations Op. 81 cl., str. 4tet & db. (*Schmidt*)

STAMITZ, C.: Quartets cl. & str. 3—Op. 8/3 & 4 (*MR*); Op. 14 (2) (or str. 4tet) (*McG & M*); Op. 19/1–3 (*MR*)

STOLZENBERG, G.: Sextet Op. 6 cl., str. 4tet & db. (*Br.*)

STRÄSSER, R.: Quintet Op. 34 cl. & str. 4tet (*Simrock*)

SIMPSON, R.: Quintet cl. & str. 4tet (*Lengnick*)

TÄGLICHSBECK, T.: Quintet Op. 44 cl. & str. 4tet (*Heinrichshofen*)

TATE, P.: Sonata cl. & vc. (*OUP*)

THILMAN, J.: Quintet Op. 73 cl. & str. 4tet (*Peters*)

WAGNER, R.: (see BAERMANN, H.)

WALTHEW, R.: Quintet cl. & str. 4tet

WANHAL (VANHALL), J.: Quartet cl. & str. 3 (*MR*); Trio Op. 20/5 cl., vn., vc. (pf.) (*Schott*)

WEBER, C. M. VON: Quintet Op. 34 cl. & str. 4tet (incl. *MR: IMC*); Introduction, Theme and Variations cl. & str. 4tet (*Lienau*)

WELLESZ, E.: Quintet Op. 81 cl. & str. 4tet (*Heinrichshofen*)

WINTER, P. VON: Quartet cl. & str. 3 (*MR*)

WORDSWORTH, W.: Quintet cl. & str. 4tet (*Lengnick*)

WURMSER, L.: Quintet cl. & str. 4tet

XENAKIS, I.: Charisma cl. & vc. (*Salabert*)

CLARINET(S) AND STRINGS WITH PIANO

ANDRIESSEN, J.: Trio cl., vc., pf. (*Donemus*)

ACHRON, J.: Children's Suite Op. 57 cl., str. 4tet & pf. (*UE*)

AMBERG, J.: Fantasiestücke Op. 12 cl., va., pf. (*Hansen*); Trio Op. 11 cl., vc., pf. (*Hansen*)

APPLEBAUM, E.: Montages cl., vc., pf. (*Chester*)
BARTÓK, B.: Contrasts cl., vn., pf. (*B & H*)
BAUSSNERN, W. VON: Serenade cl., vn., pf. (*Simrock*)
BEETHOVEN, L. VAN: Trio Op. 11 cl., vc., pf. (incl. *Peters: IMC*);
    Trio Op. 38 (composer's arr. Op. 20) cl., vc., pf. (incl.
    Peters: IMC)
BEREZOWSKY, N.: Theme & Variations, Op. 7 cl., str. 4tet & pf.
    (*Ed. Russes/B & H*)
BERG, A.: Adagio (from Chamber Concerto) cl., vn., pf. (*UE*)
BERGER, W.: Trio Op. 94 cl., vc., pf. (*MR*)
BLOMDAHL, K.-B.: Trio cl., vc., pf. (*Schott*)
BLUME, J.: Music cl., vc., pf. (*Novello*)
BRAHMS, J.: Trio Op. 114 cl. (A), vc., pf. (incl. *Peters: IMC: Br.*)
BRUCH, M.: Acht Stücke Op. 83 cl., va., pf. (*Simrock*)
COOKE, A.: Trio cl., vc., pf. (*MS.*)
COPLAND, A.: Sextet cl., str. 4tet & pf. (*B & H*)
DALBY, M.: Commedia cl., vn., vc., pf. (*Novello*)
DANKWORTH, J.: Sextet cl., str. 4tet & pf.
DOUGLAS, R.: Trio Movement cl., va., pf. (*Hin.*)
EBERL, A.: Trio Op. 36 cl., vc., pf. (*MR*)
FARRENC, L.: Trio Op. 44 cl., vc., pf. (*Leduc*)
FINNEY, R. L.: Divertissement cl., vn., vc., pf. (*Bowdoin*)
FRANKEL, B.: Trio Op. 10 cl. (A), vc., pf. (*Augener*); Pezzi Pianis-
    simi Op. 41 cl., vc., pf. (*Novello*)
FRÜHLING, C.: Trio cl., vc., pf. Op. 40 (*Leuckart*)
FORBES, S.: Partita cl., vc., pf. (*Novello*)
FELDMAN, M.: Three Clarinets, Cello & Piano (*UE*)
FINKBEINER, R.: Quartet cl., vn., vc., pf. (*Br.*)
GÁL, H.: Trio Op. 97 cl., vn., pf. (*Simrock*)
GILTAY, B.: Vier Miniaturen cl., vn., pf. (*Donemus*)
GODRON, H.: Sérénade Occidentale cl., vn., pf. (*Donemus*)
GENZMER, H.: Kammermusik cl., vn., vc., pf. (*Peters*)
GRAMATGES, H.: Trio cl., vc., pf. (*Southern*)
GROVERMANN, C. H.: Trio cl., vc., pf. (*Sander*)
HARTMAN, E.: Serenade Op. 24 cl., vc., pf. (*Simon*)
HINDEMITH, P.: Quartet cl., vn., vc., pf. (*Schott*)
HOLBROOKE, J.: Nocturne Op. 57/1 cl., va., pf. (*Chester*)
HUGHES, E.: Partita cl., vn., pf. (*MS.*)
HUBER, N.: Chronogramm cl., vn., vc., pf. (*Bosse*)
HAIK-VENTOURA, S.: Un Beau Dimanche cl., vn., pf. (*Trans-
    atlantiques*)
HAUER, J. M.: Quintet Op. 26 cl., vn., va., vc., pf. (*Lienau*)
HARRIS, R.: Concerto Op. 2 cl., str. 4tet & pf. (*Cos Cob Press*)
D'INDY, V.: Trio Op. 29 cl., vc., pf. (*Hamelle*)

IBERT, J.: Two Interludes cl., vn., pf. (hp.) (*Chester*)

IVES, C.: Largo cl., vn., pf. (*Southern*)

JUON, P.: Trio cl., vc., pf. Op. 18/3 (*Lienau*)

JACOB, G.: Trio cl., va., pf. (*MR*)

KAHN, R.: Trio Op. 45 cl., vc., pf. (*Schlesinger*)

KAMINSKI, H.: Quartet Op. 1b cl., va., vc., pf. (*UE*)

KERR, H.: Trio cl., vc., pf. (*Merion*)

KHACHATURIAN, A.: Trio cl., vn., pf. (*Peters*)

KRENEK, E.: Trio cl., vn., pf. (*AMP*)

KOETSIER, J.: Trio Op. 13/2 cl., vc., pf. (*Donemus*)

KREJCI, I.: Trio cl., db., pf. (*Artia*)

KUBICEK, A.: Trio Op. 26a cl., vc., pf. (*Doblinger*)

KARYOTAKIS, T.: Trio cl., va., pf.

KNAB, A.: Lindegger Ländler cl., vn., vc., pf. (*Schott*)

LANNOY, H. E. J. VON: Grand Trio Op. 15 cl., vc., pf. (*MR*)

LEIGHTON, K.: Trio cl., vc., pf.

LEVY, E. I.: Trio cl., vn., pf.

LEWIS, R. H.: Trio cl., vn., pf. (*Doblinger*)

MOZART, W. A.: Trio K.498 cl., va., pf. (incl. *Bä.*)

MILHAUD, D.: Suite cl., vn., pf. (*Salabert*)

MASON, D. G.: Pastorale Op. 8 cl., vn., pf. (*Salabert*)

MESSIAEN, O.: Quatuor pour la Fin du Temps cl., vn., vc., pf. (*Durand*)

MOSCHELES, I.: Fantasia Op. 46 cl., vn., vc., pf. (*MR*)

MUCZYNSKI, R.: Fantasy Trio Op. 26 cl., vc., pf.

MCCABE, J.: Sonata cl., vc., pf.

NØRGARD, P.: Trio Op. 15 cl., vc., pf. (*Hansen*)

PAYNE, A.: Paraphrases and Cadenzas cl., va., pf. (*Chester*)

POUSSEUR, H.: Quintette in memoriam Anton Webern cl., bcl., vn., vc., pf. (*Zerboni*)

PALMER, R.: Quintet cl., str. 3 & pf. (*Peer*)

PARRIS, R.: Trio cl., vc., pf. (*ACA*)

POWELL, MEL: Improvisation cl., va., pf. (*Schirmer, G.*)

PROKOFIEV, S.: Overture on Yiddish Themes cl., str. 4tet, pf. Op. 34 (*B & H*)

PETYREK, F.: Sextet cl., str. 4tet & pf. (*UE*)

PFITZNER, H.: Sextet Op. 55 cl., vn., va., vc., db. & pf. (*Oertel*)

RABL, W.: Quartet Op. 1 cl., vn., vc., pf. (*Simrock*)

REINECKE, C.: Trio Op. 264 cl. (A), va., pf. (*Simrock: IMC*); Trio Op. 274 cl., (va.)/hn., pf. (*MR*)

RIES, F.: Trio Op. 28 cl., vc., pf. (*MR*)

RIETHMÜLLER, H.: Trio Op. 46 cl., vn., pf. (*Sikorski*)

RAPHAEL, G.: Trio Op. 70 cl., vc., pf. (*Br.*)

RUDOLPH, ARCHDUKE: Trio cl., vc., pf. (*MR*)

SCHÖNBERG, A.: Suite Op. 29 cl. E♭, cl., bcl., vn., va., vc., pf. (*UE*)
SCHUMANN, R.: Märchenerzählungen Op. 132 cl., va., pf. (*Br.: IMC*)
STRAVINSKY, I.: Suite from L' Histoire du Soldat cl., vn., pf. (*Chester*)
STOKER, R.: Terzetto Op. 32 cl., va., pf. (*MS.*)
SCHROEDER, H.: Drittes Klavier-Trio Op. 43 cl. (A), vc., pf. (*Schott*)
SCOTT, C.: Trio cl., vc., pf.
SMIT, L.: Trio cl., va., pf. (*Donemus*)
STILLMAN, M.: Fantasy on a Chassidish Theme cl., str. 4tet, pf. (*Jibneh*)
SLAVICKY, K.: Trialogo cl., v., pf. (*Panton*)
SHAW, C.: Trio cl., va., pf.
SIMPSON, R.: Trio cl., vc., pf. (*Lengnick*)
SCHMIDT, F.: Quintet (in A) cl., vn., va., vc., pf. (*Weinberger*)
SCHISKE, K.: Sextet cl., str. 4tet, pf. (*UE*)
STEEL, C.: Trio fl., cl., pf.
TATE, P.: Air and Variations cl., vn., pf. (*OUP*)
UHL, F.: Kleines Konzert cl., va., pf. (*Doblinger*)
WEBERN, A.: Quartet Op. 22 vn., cl., sax., pf. (*UE*)
WANHAL (VANHALL), J.: Trio Op. 20/5 cl., vn., (vc.), pf. (*Schott*)
WALTHEW, R.: Trio cl., vn., pf. (*B & H*)
WEINGARTNER, F.: Quintet Op. 50 cl., vn., va., vc., pf. (*Br*).
WOLPE, S.: From Here on Farther cl., bcl., vn., pf.
ZEMLINSKY, A.: Trio Op. 3 cl., vc., pf. (*Simrock*)
ZILCHER, H.: Trio cl., vc., pf. (*Müller*) Op. 90

CLARINET AND OTHER WIND INSTRUMENTS
(excluding wind quintets (fl., ob., cl., hn., bn.))

ADDISON, J.: Trio ob., cl., bn. (*Joseph Williams*); Sextet fl., ob., eh., cl., bcl., bn. (*MS.*)
APOSTEL, H. E.: Quartet Op. 14 fl., cl., hn., bn (*UE*); Five Bagatelles Op. 20 fl., cl., bn. (*UE*)
ALPAERTS, F.: Evening Music 2 fl., 2 ob., 2 cl., 2 bn. (*Metropolis*)
ANDRIESSEN, J.: Respiration Suite double wind quintet incl. picc. (*Donemus*); Octuor fl., 2 ob., 2 cl., bcl., 2 bn. (*Donemus*)
ARNELL, R.: Serenade double w. 5tet & cb. (db.) (*Hin.*)
ARNOLD, M.: Divertimento Op. 37 fl., ob., cl. (*Paterson*); Trevelyan Suite 3 fl., 2 ob., 2 cl., 2 hn., 2 bn./(1 vc.) (*Faber*)
ARRIEU, C.: Trio ob., cl., bn. (*Amphion*)
AURIC, G.: Trio ob., cl., bn. (*Oiseau-Lyre*)
BACH, C. P. E.: Six Sonatas 2 fl., 2 cl., 2 hn., bn. (*MR*)
BACH, J. C.: Bläser Sinfonien 2 cl., 2 hn., 1/2 bn. (*Hofmeister*); Four 5tets 2 cl., 2 hn., bn. (*B & H*)

BADINGS, H.: Trio ob., cl., bn. (*Donemus*)

BARRAUD, H.: Trio ob., cl., bn. (*Oiseau-Lyre*)

BAVICCHI, J.: Six Duets Op. 27 fl., cl. (*OUP*)

BEETHOVEN, L. VAN: Three Duos cl., bn. (incl. *Br.: IMC*); Sextet Op. 71 2 cl., 2 hn., 2 bn. (*Br.*); Octet Op. 103 2 ob., 2 cl., 2 hn., 2 bn. (*Br.*); Rondino 2 ob., 2 cl., 2 hn., 2 bn. (*Br.*); Fidelio (arr. Sedlak) 2 ob., 2 cl., 2 hn., 2 bn., cb. (*MR*)

BAUER, M.: Duos Op. 25 ob., cl. (*Peters*)

BENNETT, R. R.: Trio fl., ob., cl. (*UE*)

BERGER, A.: Duo ob., cl. (*Peters*); Quartet fl., ob., cl., bn. (*Peters*)

BLACHER, B.: Divertimento Op. 38 fl., ob., cl., bn. (*B & B*)

BOWEN, Y.: Miniature Suite fl., ob., 2 cl., bn. (*De Wolfe*)

BOZZA, E.: Trois Mouvements fl., cl. (*Leduc*); Suite brève ob., cl., bn. (*Leduc*); Trois Pièces fl., ob., cl., bn. (*Leduc*)

BRIDGE, F.: Divertimenti fl., ob., cl., bn. (*B & H*)

BEREZOVSKY, N. T.: Suite Op. 11 fl., ob., cl., eh., bn. (*Ed. Russe*)

CARTER, E.: Eight Studies and a Fantasy fl., ob., cl., bn. (*AMP*)

CHAVEZ, C.: Solo no. 1 ob., cl., tr., bn. (*B & H*)

CASTIL-BLAZE, F. H. J.: Sextet 2 cl., 2 hn., 2 bn. (*MR*)

CHAGRIN, F.: 7 Petites Pièces picc., fl., ob., 2 cl., hn., 2 bn. (*Novello*)

COLE, H.: Serenade fl., 2 ob., 2 cl., 2 hn., 2 bn. (*Novello*)

CONSTANT, M.: Trio ob., cl., bn. (*Chester*)

CRANMER, P.: Variations on a French Tune fl., cl. (A) (*Novello*)

CROSSE, G.: Three Inventions fl., cl. (*OUP*)

CRUFT, A.: Three Bagatelles Op. 50 fl., ob., cl. (*B & H*)

CLEMENTI. A.: Tre piccoli pezzi fl., ob., cl. (*Zerboni*)

CARTAN, J.: Sonatine fl., cl. (*Heugel*)

DAVIES, P. MAXWELL: Alma Redemptoris Mater fl., ob., 2 cl., hn., bn. (*Schott*)

DANZI, F.: Sextet in E♭ 2 cl., 2 hn., 2 bn. (*Sikorski*)

DESORMIÈRE, R.: 6 Danceries du XVIème Siècle fl., eh., cl., hn., bn. (*Durand*)

DEVIENNE, F.: Trio no. 1 cl., hn., bn. (*KaWe*)

DITTERSDORF, K. DITTERS VON: Divertimento 2 ob., 2 cl., bn. (*Sikorski*)

DOMANSKY, A.: Divertimento 2 cl., hn., bn. (*Schmidt*); Quintet fl., 2 cl., hn., bn. (*Schmidt*)

DOUGLAS, R.: 6 Dance Charicatures fl., ob., cl. (*Hin.*)

DRUSCHETZKY, G.: Sestetto 2 cl., 2 hn., 2 bn. (*Schott*); 6 Partitas 2 ob., 2 cl., 2 hn., 2 bn. (*Doblinger*)

DOPPELBAUER, J. F.: incl. Trio 2 cl., bn. (*Doblinger*)

DUBOIS, P. M.: Trio ob., cl., bn. (*Leduc*); Sinfonia da Camera fl., ob., cl., alto sax/cl. 2, hn., bn. (*Leduc*)

DUBOIS, TH.: Suite no. 2, 2 fl., ob., 2 cl., hn., 2 bn. (*Leduc*)

DUVERNOY, F.: Trio no. 1 cl., hn., bn. (*KaWe*)

ENESCO, G.: Dixtuor Op. 14 2 fl., ob., eh., 2 cl., 2 hn., 2 bn. (*Enoch*)

ECKHARDT-GRAMATTÉ, S. C.: Suite fl., cl., bn. (*CMC*)

ERBSE, H.: Quartet Op. 20 fl., ob., cl., bn. (*Peters*)

ESTRADE-GUERRA, O. D': Sonatine Pastorale cl., ob. (*Jobert*)

ELER, A.-F.: 3 Quartets Op. 11 fl., cl., hn., bn. (*Leuckart*)

ETLER, A.: Suite fl., ob., cl., (*AMP*)

FERNANDEZ, O.: Two Inventions fl., cl., bn. (*Southern*); Three
    Inventions cl., bn. (*ECIC/Southern*)

FLOTHIUS, M.: incl. Quintet Op. 13 fl., ob., cl., bcl., bn. (*Donemus*)

FITELBERG, J.: Capriccio fl., ob., cl., bcl., trom./bn. (*Omega*)

FERNEYHOUGH, B.: Prometheus fl., ob., eh., cl., hn., bn. (*Peters*)

FRANÇAIX, J.: Divertissement ob., cl., bn. (*Schott*); Quatuor fl.,
    ob., cl., bn. (*Schott*)

GHENT, E.: Two Duos fl., cl./ob. (*OUP*); Quartet fl., ob. (eh.),
    cl., bn. (*OUP*)

GASSMANN, F.: Partita 2 cl., 2 hn., bn. (*Doblinger*)

GYROWETZ, A.: Serenata (2) 2 cl., 2 hn., bn. (*Heinrichshofen*)

GEBAUER, F. R.: 6 Duos Concertans Op. 8 cl., bn. (*Sikorski*)

GÁL, H.: Divertimento fl., ob., 2 cl., 2 hn., 2 bn. (*Novello*)

GOUNOD, C.: Petite Symphonie fl., 2 ob., 2 cl., 2 hn., 2 bn. (*IMC*)

GOEB, R.: Suite fl., ob., cl. (*Southern*)

GOOSSENS, E.: Fantasy fl., ob., 2 cl., 2 hn., 2 bn., tr. (*Leduc*)

HANDEL, G. F.: Overture 2 cl., bn. (*Schott*)

HAAN, S. DE: Divertimento cl., bn. (*Hin.*); Trio fl., cl., bn. (*Schott*)

HAYDN, R.: Octet 2 ob., 2 cl., 2 hn., 2 bn. (*IMC*); Divertimento
    2 cl., 2 hn. (*Doblinger/UE*)

HARVEY, P.: All at Sea ob., cl. (*New Wind Mus.*)

HEDWALL, L.: Five Epigrams fl., cl. (*Hansen*)

HINDEMITH, P.: Septet fl., ob., cl., bcl., hn., bn., tr. (*Schott*)

HODDINOT, A.: Divertimento Op. 32 ob., cl., hn., bn. (*OUP*)

HUMMEL, J. N.: Octet 2 ob., 2 cl., 2 hn., 2 bn., (cb. ad lib) (*MR*)

HOLBROOKE, J.: Serenade Op. 94 fl., ob., cl., bn. (*Blenheim*)

HUSA, K.: fl., cl., bn. Two Preludes (*Leduc*)

HOVHANESS, A.: Divertimento ob., cl., hn., bn./(3 cl., bcl.) (*Peters*)

IBERT, J.: Cinq Pièces en Trio ob., cl., bn. (*Oiseau Lyre*); Deux
    Mouvements 2 fl., cl., bn. (*Leduc*)

D'INDY, V.: Chanson et Danses Op. 50 fl., ob., 2 cl., hn., 2 bn.
    (*Durand*)

JACOB, G.: Serenade 2 fl., 2 ob., 2 cl., 2 bn. (*B & H*); Divertimento
    in E♭ 2 ob., 2 cl., 2 hn., 2 bn. (*MR*); Old Wine in New
    Bottles 2 fl. (picc.), 2 ob., 2 cl., 2 hn., 2 bn., (cb. & 2 tr. ad
    lib) (*OUP*)

JADIN, L. E.: Nocturne no. 3 fl., cl., hn., bn. (*Kneusslin*)

JANÁČEK, L.: Mládí-Suite fl. (picc.), ob., cl., bcl., hn., bn. (*Hudební/Supraphon*)

JETTEL, R.: Sextet fl., ob., 2 cl., hn., bn. (*Rubato/Doblinger*)

JOLIVET, A.: Sonatine fl., cl. (*B & H*)

JUON, P.: Arabesken Op. 73 ob., cl., bn. (*Lienau*)

JEMNITZ, A.: Trio Op. 20 fl., ob., cl. (*Zimmermann*)

JELINEK, H.: Six Aphorisms Op. 9/3 2 cl., bn. (*UE*)

JONES, DANIEL: Septet fl., ob., cl., bch., hn., bn., tr. (*MS.*)

KARG-ELERT, S.: Quintet no. 1 Op. 30 ob., 2 cl., hn., bn. (*Kahnt*); Trio Op. 49/1 ob., eh., cl. (*Hofmeister*)

KOECHLIN, C.: Trio Op. 92 fl., cl., bn. (*Salabert*); 4 Petites Pieces Op. 173 cl. (A), hn. (*Eschig*); Sonatine Modale Op. 155 fl., cl. (A) (*Eschig*); Septet Op. 165 fl., ob., eh., cl., alto sax., hn., bn. (*Oiseau Lyre*)

KRENEK, E.: Sonatina Op. 92/b fl., cl. (*Bä.*)

KROMMER, F.: Partita 2 cl., 2 hn., 2 bn. (*Hofmeister*); Octet-partitas Opp. 57, 67, 69, 79, 2 ob., 2 cl., 2 hn., 2 bn., (cb. ad lib) (*MR*)

KUBIK, G.: Little Suite fl., 2 cl. (*Hargail*)

LEWIN, G.: incl. Three Latin-American Impressions fl., cl. (*B & H*)

LUTOSLAWSKI, W.: Trio ob., cl., bn. (*PWN*)

LUTYENS, E.: Trio Op. 52 fl., cl., bn. (*Schott*); Music for Wind Op. 60 2 fl., 2 ob., 2 cl., 2 hn., 2 bn. (*Schott*)

LAJTHA, L.: Quatre Hommages Op. 42 fl., ob., cl. (A), bn. (*Leduc*)

LACHNER, F.: Octet Op. 156 fl., ob., 2 cl., 2 hn., 2 bn. (*MR*)

LANGE, G.: Nonet fl., 2 ob., 2 cl., 2 hn., 2 bn. (*Seeling*)

MALIPIERO, G. F.: Sonata à 4 fl., ob., cl., bn. (*UE*)

MARTELLI, H.: Trio Op. 45 ob., cl., bn. (*Costallat*)

MARTINON, J.: Sonatine no. 4 ob., cl., bn. (*Costallat*)

MARTINU, B.: Quatre Madrigaux ob., cl., bn. (*Eschig*)

MILHAUD, D.: Symphony no. 5 (Dixtuor d'Instruments à Vent) picc. fl., ob., eh., cl., bcl., 2 hn,. 2 bn. (*UE*); Suite d'après Corrette ob., cl., bn. (*Oiseau Lyre*)

MIRANDOLLE, L.: Quartet fl., ob., cl., bn. (*Leduc*)

MIGOT, G.: Trio ob., cl., bn. (*Leduc*)

MUSGRAVE, T.: Impromptu no. 2 fl., ob., cl. (*Chester*)

MYSLIVECEK, J.: 3 Octets 2 ob., 2 cl., 2 hn., 2 bn. (*Artia*)

MOZART, W. A.: 5 Divertimenti K. 439b 2 cl., bn. (orig. 3 bhn) (*Br.*) Divertimento no. 6 2 cl., bn. (*MR*); Adagio K.410 2 cl., bn.; Serenades K.375 & 388 2 ob., 2 cl., 2 hn., 2 bn. (*Br.*); Serenade K.361 2 ob., 2 cl., 2 bhn., 4 hn., 2 bn., cb. (db.) (*Br.*); Divertimenti K.166 & K.186 2 ob., 2 eh., 2 cl., 2 hn., 2 bn. (*Br.*)

NILSSON, BO.: incl. Gruppen picc., ob., cl. (*UE*)

NOVAČEK, R.: Sinfonietta Op. 48 fl., ob., 2 cl., 2 hn., 2 bn. (*Br.*)

OTTERLOO, W. VAN: Symphonietta voor blaasinstrumenten picc., 2 fl., 2 ob., eh., 2 cl., bcl., 4 hn., 2 bn., cb. (*Donemus*)

OLSEN, SPARNE: Suite Op. 10 fl., ob., cl. (*Lyche*)

PARRY, H.: Nonet fl., 2 ob., 2 cl., 2 hn., 2 bn. (*MS.*)

PASCAL, C.: Octet 2 fl., ob., cl., 2 hn., 2 bn., tr. (*Durand*)

PEETERS, FLOR: Trio Op. 80 fl., cl., bn. (*Hin.*)

PIERNÉ, G.: incl. Preludio e Fughetta 2 fl., ob., cl., hn., 2 bn. Op. 40/1 (*Hamelle*)

PANUFNIK, A.: Quintet fl., ob., 2 cl., bn. (*PWM*)

PIJPER, W.: Trio fl., cl., bn. (*Donemus*)

PISTON, W.: Three Pieces fl., cl., bn. (*New Music*)

POULENC, F.: Sonata cl., bn (*Chester*)

PRAAG, H. VAN: incl. Quartet fl., ob., bn. (*Donemus*); Three Sketches 2 ob., 2 cl., 2 hn., 2 bn. (*Donemus*)

PATTERSON, P.: Wind Trio fl., cl., bn. (*Weinberger*)

PLEYEL, I. J.: Quartet in E♭ fl., 2 cl., bn. (*MR*)

RAPHAEL, G.: Quartet Op. 61 fl., ob., cl., bn. (*Müller*)

RIISAGER, K.: Conversations Op. 26a ob., cl., bn. (*Engstrøm*)

REIZENSTEIN, F.: Duo ob., cl. (*Lengnick*); Trio Op. 39 fl., cl., bn. (*Lengnick*)

RIVIER, J.: Petite Suite ob., cl., bn. (*Marbot/Meridian*); Duo fl., cl. (*Billaudot*)

ROSETTI, F. A.: Quintet fl., ob., cl., eh./(hn.), bn. (*Kneusslin*); Partita 2 ob., 2 cl., 2 hn., bn. (*Kneusslin*); Partita ob., 2 cl., 2 hn., bn. (*Eulenburg*); Partita (1785) 2 fl., 2 ob., 2 cl., 2 hn., 2 bn. (db) (*OUP*)

ROSSINI, G.: Six Quartets fl., cl., hn., bn. (*Schott*)

RUEFF, J.: Three Pieces ob., cl., bn. (*Leduc*)

REINECKE, C.: Sextet Op. 271 fl., ob., cl., 2 hn., bn. (*Zimmermann*); Octet Op. 216 fl., ob., 2 cl., 2 hn., 2 bn. (*MR*)

STAMITZ, C.: Quartet Op. 8/2 ob., cl., hn., bn. (*Leuckart*)

SAUGUET, H.: Trio ob., cl., bn. (*Oiseau Lyre*)

STOCKHAUSEN, K.: Zeitmasse fl., ob., eh., cl., bn. (*UE*)

SEIBER, M.: Serenade 2 cl., 2 hn., 2 bn. (*Hansen*)

SCHMITT, F.: Lied et Scherzo 2 fl., 2 ob., 2 cl., 2 hn., 2 bn. (*Durand*)

SLAVICKY, K.: Trio ob., cl., bn. (*Hudebni*)

SUTERMEISTER, H.: incl. Serenade 2 cl., bn., tr. (*Schott*)

SZALOWSKI, A.: Duo fl., cl. (*Omega*); Trio ob., cl., bn. (*Chester*)

STRAVINSKY, I.: incl. Octet fl., cl., 2 bn., 2 tr., 2 trom. (*B & H*)

STRAUSS, R.: incl. Suite Op. 4 2 fl., 2 ob., 2d. 4 hn., 2 bn., cb. (*Leuckart*); Serenade Op. 7 2 fl., 2 ob., 2 cl. 4 hn., 2 bn., cb. (*IMC*)

TOMASI, H.: Printemps fl., ob., cl., alto sax., hn., bn. (*Leduc*); Concert Champêtre ob., cl., bn. (*Lemoine*)

TANSMAN, A., Four Impressions 2 fl., 2 ob., 2 cl., 2 bn. (*Leeds*)

TOCH, E.: Sonatinetta fl., cl., bn. Op. 84 (*Mills*)

UHL, A.: Octet 2 ob., 2 cl., 2 hn., 2 bn. (*UE*)

VILLA-LOBOS, H.: Quintet en forme de Chôros fl., ob., eh., cl., bn. (*Eschig*); Chôros no. 2 fl., cl. (*Eschig*); Trio ob., cl., bn. (*Schott*); Quartet fl., ob., cl., bn. (*Zerboni*)

VERESS, S.: Sonatina ob., cl., bn. (*Zerboni*)

WALTHEW, R. H.: Triolet ob., cl., bn. (*B & H*)

WILDGANS, F.: 3 Inventions cl., hn. (*Doblinger*); Kleines Trio fl., cl., bn. (*Doblinger*)

WEBER, C. M. VON: Adagio and Rondo 2 cl., 2 hn., 2 bn. (*MR*)

WHETTAM, G.: Divertimento no. 1 ob., cl., bn. (*De Wolfe*); Sinfonietta 2 fl., 2 ob., 2 cl., 2 hn., 2 bn. (*De Wolfe*)

ZAGWIJN, H.: incl. Trio fl., ob., cl. (*Donemus*)

WIND QUINTETS
(fl., ob., cl., hn., bn.)

ARNOLD, M.: 3 Shanties (*Paterson*)

ARRIEU, C.: (*Billaudot*)

BARBER, S.: Summer Music (*Schirmer*)

BENNETT, R. R.: (*UE*)

CAMBINI, G.: (*McG & M*)

CARTER, E.: (*AMP/Schott*)

DAMASE, J.-L.: Dix-Sept Variations Op. 22 (*Leduc*)

DANZI, F.: (8 in print) (variously *Leuckart, Kneusslin, MR*)

ETLER, A.: (*AMP*)

FARKAS, F.: Serenata (*Kultura*)

FRANÇAIX, J.: (*Schott*)

FRICKER, P. R.: (*Schott*)

GERHARD, R.: (*Mills*)

HENZE, H. W.: (*Schott*)

HINDEMITH, P.: Kleine Kammermusik Op. 24 no. 2 (incl. picc) (*Schott*)

IBERT, J.: Trois Pièces Brèves (*Leduc*)

MILHAUD, D.: La Cheminée du Roi René (*Andraud*)

MÜLLER, P.: (3) (*MR*)

NIELSEN, C.: Op. 43 (incl. eh.) (*Hansen*)

ONSLOW, G.: Op. 81/3 (*Leuckart*)

PATTERSON, P.: Comedy for 5 Winds (*Weinberger*)

REICHA, A.: (9 in print) (variously *AMP, Kneusslin, MR*)

SCHOENBERG, A.: Op. 26 (*UE*)

SEIBER, M.: Permutazioni à Cinque (*Schott*)

A comprehensive list of Wind Quintets can be found in the
Flute Repertoire Catalogue by Frans Vester (*MR*)

WIND AND PIANO

ANDRIESSEN, J.: L'Incontro di Cesare e Cleopatra fl., ob., cl., hn.,
    bn., pf. (*Donemus*)
AMBERG, J.: Suite fl., ob., cl., pf. (*Hansen*)
ARVIN, A.: Three Seasons, Suite fl., cl., pf. (*Chappell*)
BACH, C. P. E.: Six Sonatas cl., bn., pf. (*IMC*)
BEETHOVEN, L. VAN: Quintet Op. 16 ob., cl., hn., bn., pf. (*MR:
    IMC*)
BLUMER, T.: Sextet Op. 45 wind 5tet & pf. (*Simrock*)
BOISDEFFRE, R. DE: Scherzo Op. 49 wind 5tet & pf. (*Hamelle*)
BLOCH, E.: Concertino fl., cl., pf. (*Schirmer*)
CROSSE, G.: Dreamsongs ob., cl., bn., pf. (*OUP*)
COLE, H.: Trio fl., cl., pf. (*Novello*)
DANZI, F.: Quintet Op. 41 ob., cl., hn., bn., pf. (*MR: Br.*);
    Quintet Op. 53 fl., ob., cl., bn., pf. (*MR*); Quintet Op. 54
    fl., ob., cl., bn., pf. (*MR*)
DAVID, J. N.: Divertimento wind 5tet & pf. (*Br.*)
DRESDEN, SEM: incl. Petite Suite fl., ob. (eh.), cl., hn., bn., pf
    (*Donemus*)
DUVERNOY, F.: Trio no. 2 cl., hn., pf. (*KaWe*)
DONOVAN, R.: Sextet wind 5tet & pf. (*ACA*)
EMMANUEL, M.: Trio-Sonate fl., cl., pf. (*Lemoine*)
FRANÇAIX, J.: L'Heure du Berger wind 5tet & pf. (*Schott*)
GLINKA, M. I.: Trio Pathétique cl., bn., pf. (*MR*)
GHEDINI, G. F.: Concerto à Cinque fl., ob., cl., bn., pf. (*Ricordi*)
GIESEKING, W.: Quintet ob., cl., hn., bn., pf. (*B & H*)
HERZOGENBERG, H. VON: Quintet Op. 43 ob., cl., bn., hn., pf.
    (*MR: Peters*)
HOLBROOKE, J.: Sextet Op. 33a wind 5tet & pf. (*Chester: Blenheim*)
HONEGGER, A.: Rhapsody 2 fl., cl., pf. (*Salabert*)
HURLESTONE, W.: Trio cl., bn., pf. (*MS.*)
HARTZELL, E.: Trio fl., bcl., pf. (*Doblinger*)
JACOB, G.: Sextet fl. (picc.), ob. (eh.), cl., hn., bn., pf. (*MR*)
JUON, P.: Divertimento wind 5tet & pf. (*Schlesinger*)
KOPPEL, H.: Sextet wind 5tet & pf. Op. 36 (*Skandinavisk*)
KURI-ALDANA, M.: Cantares fl., cl., pf. (*MR*)
KREUTZER, C.: Trio Op. 43 cl., bn., pf. (*Hofmeister*)
LEEUW, TON DE: Trio fl., cl., pf. (*Donemus*)

LUTYENS, E.: Fantasie-Trio Op. 55 fl., cl., pf. (*UE*)

LLOYD, CH.: Trio cl., bn., pf. (*Rudall Carte/B & H*)

MAW, N.: Chamber Music ob., cl., hn., bn., pf. (*Chester*)

MARTINU, B.: Sextet fl., ob., cl., 2 bn., pf. (*Panton*)

MENDELSSOHN, F.: Zwei Konzertstücke Opp. 113 & 114 cl., bhn., pf. (*Br./IMC*)

MILHAUD, D.: Sonata fl., ob., cl., pf. (*Durand*)

MOZART, W. A.: Quintet K.452 ob., cl., hn., bn., pf. (*MR: IMC: Bä.*)

PIJPER, W.: Sextet wind 5tet & pf. (*Donemus*)

PLEYEL. I. J.: Quintet ob., cl., hn., bn., pf. (*MR*)

POSTON, E.: Trio fl., cl., pf./(hp.) (*Chester*)

POULENC, F.: Sextuor wind 5tet & pf. (*Hansen*)

RAWSTHORNE, A.: Quintet ob., cl., hn., bn., pf. (*OUP*)

REGT, H. DE: Musica per 6 strumenti a fiato e clavicembalo Op. 26 2 fl., 2 cl., 2 bn., pf. (*Donemus*)

REINECKE, C.: Trio Op. 274 cl., hn./(va.), pf. (*MR*)

RIMSKY-KORSAKOV, N.: Quintet fl., cl., hn., bn., pf. (*IMC*)

ROUSSEL, A.: Divertissement Op. 6 wind 5tet & pf. (*Rouart*)

RUBINSTEIN, A.: Quintet Op. 55 fl., cl., hn., bn., pf. (*Hamelle*)

SAINT-SAËNS, C.: Tarantelle Op. 6 fl., cl., pf. (*Durand*); Caprice Op. 79 fl., ob., cl., pf. (*Durand*)

SCHMITT, F.: A Tour d'Anches Op. 97 ob., cl., bn., pf. (*Durand*); Sonatine en Trio fl., cl., pf. Op. 85 (*Durrand*)

SHOSTAKOVICH, D.: 4 Waltzes fl., cl., pf. (*MR*)

SMIT, L.: Sextuor wind 5tet & pf. (*Donemus*)

SPOHR, L.: Quintet Op. 52 fl., cl., hn., bn., pf. (*Bä.: MR*)

SUGÁR, R.: Frammenti musicali wind 5tet & pf. (*EMB*)

SYDEMAN, W.: Trio bcl., bn., pf. (*Okra*)

TCHEREPNIN, I.: Cadenzas in Transition fl., cl., pf. (*Belaieff/B & H*)

THUILLE, L.: Sextet Op. 6 wind 5tet P pf. (*Br.*)

TON-THAT, TIÊT: Quatre Grands Paysages fl., ob., cl., bn., pf. (*Transatlantiques*)

TOVEY, D. F.: Trio Op. 8 cl., hn., pf. (*Schott*)

TANSMAN, A.: La Danse de la Sorcière wind 5tet & pf. (*Eschig*)

VILLA-LOBOS, H.: Fantasie Concertante cl., bn., pf. (*Eschig*)

WILLIAMSON, M.: Pas de Quatre fl., ob., cl., bn., pf. (*Weinberger*)

WHETTAM, G.: Fantasy Sextet wind 5tet & pf. (*De Wolfe*)

ZAGWIJN, H.: Trio ob., cl., pf. (*Donemus*); Suite wind 5tet & pf. (*Donemus*); Scherzo wind 5tet & pf. (*Donemus*)

WIND AND STRINGS

ANDRIESSEN, J.: Hommage à Milhaud wind 5tet, tr., trom., sax., str. 3 (*Donemus*)

ARNOLD, M.: Trevelyan Suite 3 fl., 2 ob., 2 cl., 2 hn., vc./(2 bn.) (*Faber*)

BACH, W. F.: Sextet cl., 2 hn., str. 3 (*Litolff*)

BADINGS, H.: Octet cl., hn., bn., str. 4tet, db. (*Donemus*)

BEETHOVEN, L. VAN: Septet Op. 20 cl., hn., bn., str., 3, db. (incl. *Peters*)

BENTZON, J.: Variazioni Interrotti Op. 12 cl. bn., str. 3 (*Hansen*)

BERKELEY, L.: Sextet Op. 47 cl., hn., str. 4tet (*Chester*)

BERWALD, F.: Septet cl., hn., bn., str. 3, db. (*Suecia*)

BLACHER, B.: Oktett cl., hn., bn., str. 4tet, db. (*B & B*)

BUTTERWORTH, A.: Modal Suite fl., cl., bn., tr., vn. (*Hin.*)

CASELLA, A.: Serenata cl., bn., tr., vn., vc. (*UE*)

CROSSE, G.: Villanelles for 7 Instruments wind 5tet, vn., vc. (*OUP*)

DESSAU, P.: Concertino vn., fl., cl., hn. (*Schott*)

DUBOIS, T.: Nonet fl., ob., cl., bn., str. 4tet, db. (*Heugel*)

DVOŘÁK, A.: Serenade Op. 44 2 ob., 2 cl., 3 hn., 2 bn., vc., db. (*MR: IMC*)

EISLER, H.: Suite Op. 92a (Variations on American Nursery Rhymes) fl. (picc), cl., bn., str. 4tet (*Neue Musik/Br.*); Septet no. 2 fl. (picc.), cl., bn., str. 4tet (*Br.*); Nonet no. 1 (*Variations*) fl., cl., hn., bn., str. 4tet, db. (*Peters*)

ETLER, A.: Quartet ob., cl., va., bn. (*Valley*)

FERGUSON, H.: Octet cl., hn., bn., str. 4tet, db. (*B & H*)

FLOTHUIS, M.: Divertimento Op. 46 cl., hn., bn., vn., va., db. (*Donemus*)

FRICKER, P. R.: Octet Op. 30 fl., cl., hn., bn., str. 3, db. (*Schott*)

FRANÇAIX, J.: Octuor cl., hn., bn., str. 4tet, db. (*Schott*)

HAAN, S. DE: Suite ob., vn., cl., vc. (*Hin*).

HARBISON, J.: Serenade fl. (picc.), cl., bcl., str. 3 (*MS.*)

HARTLEY, W. S.: Divertimento fl., ob., cl., hn., bn., vc. (*Fema*)

HINDEMITH, P.: Octet cl., hn., bn., vn., 2 va., vc., db. (*Schott*)

HARSÁNYI, T.: Nonet fl., ob., cl., hn., bn., str. 4tet (*La Sirène*)

HOMS, J.: Trio fl., vn., bcl.

IRELAND, J.: Sextet cl., hn., str. 4tet (*Augener*)

KAMINSKI, H.: Quintet cl., hn., str. 3 (*UE*)

KREUTZER, C.: Grand Septet Op. 62 cl., hn., bn., str. 3, db. (*MR: UE*)

LANDRÉ, G.: Sextet fl., cl., str. 4tet (*Donemus*)

LEEUW, TON DE: 5 Sketches ob., cl., bn., str. 3 (*Donemus*)

LUTOSLAWSKI, W.: Dance Preludes (version 1959) fl., ob., cl., hn., bn., str. 3, db. (*Hansen*)

MARTINU, B.: Nonet fl., ob., cl., hn., bn., str. 3, db. (*Artia*); Serenata no. 1 cl., hn., 3 vn., va. (*Artia*)

MIRANDOLLE, L.: Octet cl., hn., bn., str. 4tet, db. (*MS.*)

MOSS, L.: Windows fl., cl., db. (*MS.*)

MUSGRAVE, T.: Chamber Concerto no. 3 cl., hn., bn., str. 4tet, db. (*Chester*)

MILHAUD, D.: Aspen Serenade fl., ob., cl., bn., tr., str. 3, db. (*Heugel*)

MOZART, W. A.: Serenade K.361 2 ob., 2 cl., 2 bhn., 4 hn., 2 bn., db. (incl. *MR*)

MASSENET, J.: Introduction and Variations Wind 5tet and str. 4tet (*Heugel*)

NIELSEN, C.: Serenata-Invano cl., hn., bn., vc., db. (*Skandinavisk*)

NIEHAUS, M.: Sextet cl., hn., bn., vn., va., db. (*MS.*)

PONSE, L.: Quintet fl., ob., cl., va., vc. (*Donemus*)

PRAAG, H. C. VAN: incl. Dixtuor fl., ob., cl., hn., bn., str. 4tet, db. (*Donemus*)

PROKOVIEV, S.: Quintet Op. 39 ob., cl., vn., va., db. (*IMC*)

POULENC, F.: Mouvements Perpetuels (arr. by the composer) fl., ob., cl., hn., bn., str. 3, db. (*Chester*)

PISK, P.: Music vn., cl., vc., bn. (*CFE*)

REICHA, A.: Octet Op. 96 ob./(fl.), cl., hn., bn., str.4 tet, (db. ad lib) (*MR*)

RHEINBERGER, J.: Nonet Op. 139 fl., ob., cl., hn., bn., str. 3, db. (*MR*)

RIISAGER, K.: Sonata fl., cl., vn., vc. (*Hansen*)

ROSETTI, A.: Partita (1785) 2 fl., 2 ob., 2 cl., 3 hn., 2 bn., db. (*OUP*)

SEARLE, H.: Quartet Op. 12 vn., va., cl., bn. (*Lyche/Hin.*)

SKALKOTTAS, N.: Octet fl., ob., cl., bn., str. 4tet (*MS.*)

SCHIDLOWSKY, L.: Cuerteto mixto fl., cl., vn., vc. (*IEM*)

SCHOLLUM, R.: Octet Op. 63 fl., ob., cl., bn., str. 3, db. (*Doblinger*)

SCHUBERT, F.: Octet Op. 166 cl., hn., bn., str. 4tet, db. (*Peters: IMC*)

SPOHR, L.: Nonet Op. 31 fl., ob., cl., hn., bn., str. 3, db. (*Litolff/Peters*); Octet Op. 32 cl., 2 hn., vn., 2 va., vc., db. (*MR*)

STRAVINSKY, I.: Pastorale vn., ob., eh., cl. (A), bn. (*Schott*)

STANFORD, C. V.: Serenade Op. 95 fl., cl., bn., hn., str. 3, db. (*Stainer & Bell*)

STRAUSS, R. (arr. HASENÖHRL): Till Eulenspiegel einmal anders! vn., cl., hn., bn., db. (*Peters*)

STEVENS, H.: Septet cl., hn., bn., 2 va., 2 vc. (*ACA*)

THOMSON, R.: Suite ob., cl., va. (*Schirmer*)

THOMSON, V.: Sonata da chiesa cl. E♭, tr., va., hn., trom. (*New Music*)

TREMBLAY, GEO.: Quartet ob., cl., va., bn. (*Christlieb*)

TIESSEN, H.: Amsel Septett Op. 20 fl., cl., hn., str. 4tet (*Ries & Erler*)

TURCHI, G.: Trio fl., cl., va. (*Hin.*)

VARÈSE, E.: Octandre fl., ob., cl., hn., bn., tr., trom., db. (*Colfrank/Ricordi*)

VILLA-LOBOS, H.: Chôros no. 7 fl., ob., cl., sax., bn., vn., vc. (*Eschig*)

VOGEL, W.: 12 Variétudes vn., fl., cl., vc. (*Zerboni*)

WELLESZ, E.: Octet Op. 67 cl., hn., bn., str. 4tet, db. (*Lengnick*)

WAGNER, R.: Siegfried Idyll fl., ob., 2 cl., bn., 2 hn., tr. str. 4tet, db. (*Br.*)

WIRÉN, DAG: Quartet Op. 31 fl., ob., cl., vc. (*Gehrmans*)

WYNER, Y.: Passover Offering fl., cl., trom., vc. (*AMP*)

WOOLDRIDGE, K.: 3 Pieces vc., fl., ob., cl., bn. (*De Wolfe*)

XENAKIS, I.: Anaktoria cl., hn., bn., str. 4tet, db. (*Salabert*)

YUN, I.: Music for 7 Instruments fl., ob., cl., hn., bn., vn., vc. (*B & B*)

ZILLIG, W.: Serenade no. 2 cl., E♭, cl. (A), bcl., cornet, tr., trom., str. 3 (*Bä.*)

WIND, WITH OR WITHOUT STRINGS, AND OTHER INSTRUMENTS NOT INCLUDED IN OTHER CATEGORIES

ADDISON, J.: Serenade wind 5tet & hp. (*OUP*)

APIVOR, D.: Concertante cl., pf., 2 perc.

AURIC, G.: 5 Bagatelles cl., bn., tr., vn., vc., pf. (*Andraud*)

BRINDLE, R. SMITH: Concerto à 5 & percussion fl. (picc.), cl. (bcl.), vib., hp., pf., perc. (*Hin.*)

BANKS, D.: Sonata da Camera fl., cl., bcl., str. 3, pf., perc. (*Schott*)

BAX, A.: Nonet fl., ob., cl., str. 4tet, db., hp. (*Chappell*)

BIRTWISTLE, H.: 'The World is Discovered' 2 fl., ob., eh., cl., bhn./bcl., 2 hn., 2 bn., hp., guitar (*UE*)

BROWN, EARLE: Pentathis for 9 Solo Instruments fl., bcl., tr., trom., vn., va., vc., hp., pf. (*Schott*)

BURGE, D.: Sources III cl., perc. (*Broude-A.*)

CASELLA, A.: Sinfonia Op. 54 cl., tr., va., pf. (*Carisch*)

CASTIGLIONI, N.: incl. Tropi fl., cl., vn., vc., perc. (*Zerboni*)

CHEMIN-PETIT, H. H.: Short Suite ob., cl., bn., str. 4tet, db., timp. (*Hin.*)

COOKE, A.: Quartet fl., cl., vc., pf. (*MS.*)

DAVIES, P. MAXWELL: Sextet fl., cl., bcl., vn., vc., pf. (*Schott*); Ricercar and Doubles on 'To Many a Well' wind 5tet, va., vc., harpsichord (*Schott*); Antechrist picc., bcl., vn., vc., 3 perc. (*B & H*); Stedman Doubles cl. & perc. (*B & H*)

DOHNANYI, E.: Sextet Op. 37 cl., hn., str. 3, pf. (*Lengnick*)

DONATONI, F.: For Grilly—improvisations for fl., cl., bcl., str. 3, perc. (*Zerboni*); 'Etwas ruhiger im Ausdruck' fl., cl., vn., vc., pf. (*Zerboni*)

DUNHILL, T.: Quintet Op. 3 cl., hn., vn., vc., pf. (*Rudall Carte/B & H*)

EISLER, H.: Quintet Op. 70 fl., cl., vn./va., vc., pf. (*Litolff*); Nonet (no. 2) fl., cl., bn., tr., perc., 3 vn., db. (*Neue Musik/Br.*)

FIBICH, Z.: Quintet Op. 42 cl., hn., vn., vc., pf. (*Urbánek*)

FALLA, M. DE: Concerto fl., ob., cl., vn., vc., harpsichord (*Eschig*)

GERHARD, R.: Libra fl., cl., vn., guitar, pf., perc. (*OUP*)

GENZMER, H.: Septet fl., cl., hn., str. 3, hp. (*Schott*)

GHEDINI, G. F.: Adagio e Allegro da Concerto fl., cl., hn., str. 3, hp. (*Ricordi*)

GOEHR, A.: Suite Op. 11 fl., cl., hn., vn., vc., hp. (*Schott*)

GILBERT, A.: O'Grady Music cl., vc., & toy instr.

HINDEMITH, P.: Drei Stücke cl., tr., vn., db., pf. (*Schott*)

HODDINOTT, A.: Septet Op. 10 cl., hn., bn., str. 3, pf. (*MS.*)

HUMMEL, J. N.: Septet Militaire Op. 114 fl., cl., tr., vn., vc., db., pf. (*MR*)

IBERT, J.: Two Interludes cl., vn., hp.(pf.) (*Chester*); Capriccio fl., ob., cl., bn., tr., str. 4tet, hp. (*Leduc*); Le Jardinier de Samos fl., cl., tr., vn., vc., perc. (*Heugel*)

INGENHOVEN, J.: Trio fl., cl., hp (*Salabert*)

JANÁČEK, L.: Concertino cl. (E♭ & B♭), hn., bn., 2 vn., va., pf. (*Hudebni*)

JUON, P.: Octet Op. 27 ob., cl., hn., bn., str. 3, pf. (*Schlesinger*)

KILAR, W.: Training 68 cl., vc., trom., pf. (*PWM*)

KOPELENT, M.: Music for 5 ob., cl., bn., vn., pf. (*Gerig*)

KROEGER, K.: Toccata cl., trom., perc. (*Broude-A*)

KLEBE, G.: 7 Bagatelles bhn., trom., hp., tubular bell (*B & B*)

LUCAS, L.: Rhapsody 2 fl., 2 cl., str. 4tet, hp. (*MS*)

LUTYENS, E.: Concerto Grosso Op. 8/5 cl., sax., str. 4tet, pf. (*Chester*); 6 Tempi for 10 Instruments Op. 42 wind 5tet, tr., str. 3, pf. (*Mills*)

LACHENMANN, H. F.: Trio fluido cl., va., marimbaphone (*Gerig*)

MACONCHY, E.: Reflections ob., cl., vn., hp. (*OUP*)

MARTINU, B.: La Revue de Cuisine cl., bn., tr., vn., vc., pf. (*Leduc*)

MIGOT, G.: incl. Quartet fl., cl., vn., hp. (*Leduc*)

MUSGRAVE, T.: Serenade fl., cl., va., vc., hp. (*Chester*); Chamber Concerto no. 2 fl., cl., vn., vc., pf. (*Hansen*)

MOLNAR, A.: Serenata cl., vn., hp. (*Zerboni*)

MALOVEC, J.: Cryptogram bcl., pf., perc. (*Supraphon*)

NONO, L.: Polifonia-Monodia-Ritmica fl., cl., bcl., sax., hn., pf., perc. (*Schott*)

ONSLOW, G.: incl. Grand Sextuor Op. 77 bis fl., cl., hn., bn., db., pf. (*Heugel*)

PETRASSI, G.: Sonata da Camera fl., ob., cl., bn., 2 vn., 2 va., vc., db., harpsichord (*Zerboni*)

PROSPERI, C.: Four Inventions cl., vn., va., hp.

PAZ, J. C.: Dédalus fl., cl., vn., vc., pf. (*ECA*)

POUSSEUR, H.: Madrigal 3 cl., vn., vc., pf., 2 perc. (*UE*)

PIJPER, W.: Septet wind 5tet, db., pf. (*Donemus*)

POLOLÁNIK, z.: Musica Spingenta no. 3 bcl., 13 perc. (*Panton*)

PINOS, A.: Conflicts bcl., vn., pf., perc. (*Panton*)

RAVEL, M.: Introduction and Allegro fl., cl., str. 4tet, hp. (*Durand*)

RUBINSTEIN, A.: Octet Op. 9 fl., cl., hn., vn., va., vc., pf. (*Peters*)

REGAMEY, C.: Quintet cl., bn., vn., vc., pf. (*PWM*)

ROCHBERG, G.: Contra mortem et tempus fl., cl., vn., pf. (*Presser*); Electra kaleidoscope fl., cl., vn., vc., pf.

RUYNEMAN, D.: Divertimento fl., cl., hn., va., pf. (*Chester*)

RAWSTHORNE, A.: Quintet cl., hn., vn., vc., pf. (*OUP*)

RUSSELL, A.: Pas de Deux cl., perc. (*Mus. for Perc., NY*)

REINER, K.: Trio fl., bcl., perc. (*Supraphon*)

SAUGUET, H.: Près du Bal fl., cl., bn., vn., pf. (*Rouart*)

SCHAT, P.: Septet fl., ob., bcl., hn., vc., pf., perc. (*Donemus*)

SHEINKMAN, M.: Divertimento cl., tr., trom., hp. (*Hin.*)

SPINNER, L.: Quintet cl., hn., bn., db., guitar (*B & H*)

SPOHR, L.: Septet Op. 147 fl., cl., hn., bn., vn., vc., pf. (*MR*)

STRAESSER, J.: Encounters bcl., 6 perc. (*Donemus*)

SCULTHORPE, P.: Tabuh Tabuhan wind 5tet & perc. (*Faber*)

SHIFRIN, S.: Serenade for 5 Instruments ob., cl., vn., hn., pf. (*Peters*)

STIBILJ, M.: Zoom cl. & bongos (*Bä.*)

SYDEMAN, W.: Quartet fl., cl., vn., pf. (*Okra*)

SZALONEK, W.: Improvisations sonoristiques cl., trom., vc., pf. (*PWM*)

STRAVINSKY, I.: Septet cl., hn., bn., str. 3, pf. (*B & H*); Epitaphium fl., cl., hp. (*B & H*)

SCHOENBERG, A.: Chamber Symphony Op. 9 arr. Webern fl., cl., vn., vc., pf. (*UE*)

STOCKHAUSEN, K.: Kreuzspiel ob., bcl., pf., 3 perc. (*UE*)

SKALKOTTAS, N.: Andante sostenuto fl., ob., eh., cl., bn., cb., hn., tr., trom., tuba, timpani, perc., pf. (*UE*)

TAILLEFERRE, G.: Images fl., cl., str. 4tet, pf., celeste (*Chester*)

TOCCHI, G. L.: Arlecchino—Divertimento fl., cl., str. 3, hp. (*Schott*)

TOCH, E.: Dance Suite Op. 30 fl., cl., vn., va., db., perc. (*Schott*)

WHETTAM, G.: Septet fl., cl., str. 4tet, hp.

WEBERN, A.: Concerto Op. 24 fl., ob., cl., hn., tr., trom., vn., va., pf. (*UE*)

WERNICK, R.: Stretti cl., vn., va., guitar (*Mills*)
WESTERGAARD, P.: Quartet cl., vn., vc., vib. (*Schott*)

CLARINET(S), WITH OR WITHOUT OTHER INSTRUMENTS, AND TAPE
(including pre-recorded tape)

BERIO, L.: Différences fl., cl., va., vc., hp. & tape (*Zerboni*)
BIRTWISTLE, H.: Linoi 2 cl. & tape (*UE*); Interludes bhn. & tape
DRUCKMAN, J.: Animus 3 cl. & tape (*MCA*)
DIEMENTE, E.: Mirrors 5 cl. & tape
HAYNES, STANLEY: Extensions cl. & tape (*Chester*)
LEEUW, TON DE: Antiphonie fl., ob., cl., hn., bn. & 4-track tape (*Donemus*)
NEWSON, GEORGE: Alan's Piece Again cl. & 4-track tape
PERT, MORRIS: Akhenaten cl. Eb, cl. Bb, bcl. & tape (*Weinberger*)
PATTERSON, P.: Shadows cl. & tape (*Weinberger*)
ROXBURGH, E.: Monologue for Alan Hacker cl. & tape
SMALLEY, DENIS: Anaphora 1 cl. & tape
SUBOTNICK, M.: Serenade 3 fl., cl., vn., pf. & tape (*Bowdoin*)
VEGA, A. DE LA: Interpolation cl. & tape (*STA*)

VOICE(S) WITH NOT MORE THAN FOUR INSTRUMENTS INCLUDING CLARINET(S)

ABERCROMBIE, A.: Songs of Solitude sop., cl., pf.
AMY, G.: D'un desastre obscur mezzo & cl. (A) (*UE*)
APOSTEL, H. E.: Lieder Op. 22 med. voice, fl., cl., bn. (*UE*)
BABBITT, M.: 2 Sonnets bar., cl., va., vc. (*AMP*)
BECKWITH, J.: The Great Lakes Suite sop., bar., cl., vc., pf.
BERIO, L.: Chamber Music sop., cl., vc., hp. (*Zerboni*); Agnus 2 sop., 3 cl. (*UE*)
BIRTWISTLE, H.: Ring a Dumb Carillon sop., cl., pf. (*UE*)
BLISS, A.: Two Nursery Rhymes sop., cl., pf. (*Chester*)
BALASSA, S.: Antinomia mezzo, cl., vc.
COOKE, A.: Three Songs of Innocence, sop., cl., pf. (*OUP*)
COPLAND, A.: 'As it fell upon a day' voice, fl., cl. (*New Mus.*)
COWIE, E.: Shinkohinshu sop., fl., cl., pf.
CRUMB, G.: Echos 1–11 Echos of Autumn 1965 alto, fl., cl., vn., pf. (*Mills*)
DALLAPICCOLA, L.: Goethe-Lieder mezzo, cl. Eb, cl. Bb, bcl. (*Zerboni*); Due Liriche di Anacreonte sop., cl. Eb, cl. A, va., pf. (*Zerboni*)
DALBY, M.: Cantica sop., cl., va., pf.

DAVIES, H.: Vom ertrunkenen Mädchen sop., fl., cl., pf.

EISLER, H.: incl. Palmström Op. 5 voice, fl., cl., vn. (*UE*)

FELDMAN, M.: Journey to the End of Night sop., fl., cl., bcl., bn. (*Peters*)

FRICKER, P. R.: Come Sleep contralto, alto fl., bcl.

GIDEON, M.: Rhymes from the Hill voice, cl., vc., marimba (*CFE*)

HAMILTON, I.: Songs of Summer Op. 27a sop., cl., pf.

HOOK, J.: 3 Songs sop., cl., pf. (*Schott*)

HOVHANESS, A.: Saturn sop., cl., pf. (*Peters*)

HORVATH, J. M.: 4 Lieder sop./tenor, fl., cl., va., vc. (*Peters*)

JACOB, G.: Three Songs sop., cl. (*OUP*)

JOSEPHS, W.: Four Japanese Lyrics sop., cl., pf. (*Novello*)

KAMINSKI, H.: 3 Sacred Songs voice., vn. (*UE*)

KNUSSEN, O.: Rosary Songs sop., cl., va., pf.

KOLB, B.: 3 Place Settings narrator, cl., vn., db., perc. (*Fischer*)

LLOYD, C.: Annette bar., cl., pf. (*Novello*)

MCCABE, J.: 3 Folk Songs sop., cl., pf. (*Novello*)

MELLERS, W.: Carmina filium voice, cl., vn., vc., pf.

MOZART, W. A.: 'Parto' (La Clemenza di Tito) arr. voice, cl., pf. (*Schott*); Four Notturni K.346, 436, 439, 549 2 sop. & bass, 3 bhn. (*Br.*) Two Notturni K.437, 438 2 sop. & bass, 2 cl., bhn. (*Br.*)

MUSGRAVE, T.: Four Portraits bar., cl., pf. (*Chester*)

NOVÁK, J.: Mimus Magicus sop., cl., pf. (*Zanibon*)

RIDOUT, A.: Hölderlinlieder sop., cl. (*Chappell*)

RORAM, N.: Ariel sop., cl., pf. (*B & H*)

ROUTH, F.: Circles sop., cl., va., pf.

SMIT, L.: Academia Graffiti voice, cl., vc., pf., perc. (*Mills*)

STEVENS, H.: 2 Shakespeare Songs voice, fl., cl. (*ACA*)

SHAW, C.: Sonnet tenor, cl.

SCHUBERT, F.: Der Hirt auf dem Felsen sop., cl., pf. (*Br.*)

SEIBER, M.: Morgenstern-Lieder sop., cl. (*UE*)

SPOHR, L.: Deutsche Lieder Op. 103 sop., cl., pf. (*Bä.*)

STRAVINSKY, I.: Berceuses du Chat contralto, 3 cl. (Eb, Bb, A) (*Chester*); Three Songs from Shakespeare mezzo, fl., cl., va. (*B & H*); Elegy for J.F.K. bar., 2 cl. (Bb), alto cl. (*B & H*)

TEED, R.: 5 Funny Songs bar., cl., pf.

VAUGHAN WILLIAMS, R.: Three Vocalises sop., cl. (*OUP*)

VILLA-LOBOS, H.: Poêma da Criança e sua Mamâ voice, fl., cl., vc. (*Eschig*)

WEBERN, A.: Six Songs Op. 14 sop., vn., cl., bcl., vc. (*UE*); Five Canons Op. 16 sop., cl., bcl. (*UE*); Three Folksongs Op. 17 voice, vn., va., cl., bcl. (*UE*); Three Songs Op. 18 voice, cl. Eb, guitar (*UE*)

WARD-STEINMAN, D.: Fragments from Sappho sop., fl., cl., pf. (*Marks*)

WELLESZ, E.: The Leaden Echo and the Golden Echo sop., vn., cl., vc., pf. (*Schott*)

WOLPE, S.: Street Music bar., ob., cl., vc., pf. (*BCMA*)

WILKINSON, M.: Voices contralto, fl., cl. E♭, bcl., vc. (*UE*)

The following composers have written works for voice and larger groups of instruments, including clarinet:

D. Bedford, L. Berio, A. Bliss, L. Durey, W. Fortner, R. Gerhard, F. García, Y. Hachimura, H. W. Henze, W. Lutoslawski, E. Lutyens, W. Mellers, D. Milhaud, F. Poulenc, A. Panufnik, R. Pleskow, M. Ravel, H. Sauguet, M. Schafer, I. Stravinsky, A. Schoenberg, R. Stewart, P. Tate, W. Walton (Façade-OUP), A. Webern, K. Weill